Sir Arthur Conan Doyle's

THE ADVENTURES OF
SHERLOCK HOLMES

Other Avon Camelot Books
in the series:

Sir Arthur Conan Doyle's
THE ADVENTURES OF SHERLOCK HOLMES
adapted by
Catherine Edwards Sadler

BOOK ONE:
A Study in Scarlet
The Red-headed League
The Man with the Twisted Lip

BOOK TWO:
The Sign of the Four
The Adventure of the Blue Carbuncle
The Adventure of the Speckled Band

BOOK THREE:
The Adventure of the Engineer's Thumb
The Adventure of the Beryl Coronet
The Adventure of Silver Blaze
The Adventure of the Musgrave Ritual

Sir Arthur Conan Doyle's
THE ADVENTURES OF
SHERLOCK HOLMES

BOOK FOUR

The Adventure of the Reigate Puzzle
The Adventure of the Crooked Man
The Adventure of the Greek Interpreter
The Adventure of the Naval Treaty

Adapted for young readers by
CATHERINE EDWARDS SADLER

Illustrated by ANDREW GLASS

AN AVON CAMELOT BOOK

5th grade reading level has been determined by using the Fry Readability Scale.

SIR ARTHUR CONAN DOYLE'S THE ADVENTURES OF SHERLOCK
HOLMES adapted by Catherine Edwards Sadler is an original publication of
Avon Books. This work has never before appeared in book form.

AVON BOOKS
A division of
The Hearst Corporation
105 Madison Avenue
New York. New York 10016

Copyright © 1981 by Catherine Edwards Sadler
Text illustrations Copyright © 1981 by Andrew Glass
Cover illustration by Howard Levitt
Book design by Joyce Kubat
Published by arrangement with the author
Library of Congress Catalog Card Number: 81-65084
ISBN: 0-380-78113-1

First Avon Camelot Printing: November 1981

Sadler, Catherine Edwards.
    Sir Arthur Conan Doyle's The Adventures of Sherlock Holmes.

    (An Avon Camelot Book)
    Contents: Bk. 1. A study in scarlet. The red-headed league. The man
with the twisted lip — Bk. 2 The sign of the four. The adventure of the
blue carbuncle. The adventure of the speckled band — Bk. 3. The
adventure of the engineer's thumb. The adventure of the beryl
coronet. The adventure of silver blaze. The adventure of the Musgrave
ritual — [etc.]
    1. Detective and mystery stories, American.
    2. Children's stories, American. [1. Mystery and detective stories.
    2. Short stories] I. Glass, Andrew, ill.

    II. Doyle, Arthur Conan, Sir, 1859-1930. Adventures of Sherlock
Holmes. III. Title. IV. Title: Adventures of Sherlock Holmes.
PZ7.S1238Si   [Fic]   81-65084
                        AACR2

Table of Contents

Introduction

Sir Arthur Conan Doyle was born in Edinburgh, Scotland, on May 22, 1859. In 1876 he entered the Edinburgh Medical College as a student of medicine. There he met a certain professor named Joseph Bell. Bell enjoyed amusing his students in a most unusual way. He would tell them a patient's medical and personal history before the patient had uttered a single word! He would observe the exact appearance of the patient and note the smallest detail about him: marks on his hands, stains on his clothing, the jewelry he wore. He would observe a tattoo, a new gold chain, a worn hat with unusual stains upon it. From these *observations* he would then make *deductions*. In other words, he would come to conclusions by reasoning in a logical manner. For example, a tattoo and the way a man walked could lead to the deduction that the man had been to sea; a new gold chain could lead to the deduction that he had come into recent wealth. Time and time again Professor Bell's deductions proved correct!

Conan Doyle was intrigued by Professor Bell's skills of observation and deduction. Since his early youth he had been fascinated by the mysterious. He loved mysteries and detective stories. He himself had already tried his hand at writing. Now a new sort of hero began to take shape in Conan Doyle's mind. His hero would be a detective—not just an ordinary detective, though. No, he would be extraordinary... a man like Bell who observed the smallest detail. He would take his skills of observation and work them out to an exact science—the science of deduction. "It is all very well to say that a man is clever," Conan Doyle wrote, "but the reader wants to see examples of it—such examples as Bell gave us every day. . . ." So Conan Doyle created just such a clever man, a man who had perfected the skill of observation, turned it into an exact science, and then used it as the basis of his career. His cleverness would be revealed in the extraordinary methods he used to solve his cases and capture his criminals.

Little by little the personality and world of his new character took shape. At last he became the sharp-featured fellow we all know as Mr. Sherlock Holmes. Next Conan Doyle turned his imagination to Holmes' surroundings—those "comfortable rooms in Baker Street"—where the fire was always blazing and where footsteps were always heard on the stair. And then there was Watson, dear old Watson! He was much like Conan Doyle himself, easygoing, typically British, a doctor and a writer. Watson would be Holmes' sidekick, his friend and his chronicler. He would be humble and admiring, always asking Holmes to explain his theories, always ready to go out into the foggy, gaslit streets of London on some mysterious mission. All that remained to create were the adventures themselves.

Taking up his pen in 1886, Conan Doyle set to work on a short novel, or novella as it is sometimes called. He finished *A Study in Scarlet* in just two months. It was the first of sixty Sherlock Holmes stories to come and it began a career for Dr. Arthur Conan Doyle that would eventually win him a knighthood.

Today Holmes is considered one of—if not *the*—most popular fictional heroes of all time. More has been written about this character than any other. Sherlock Holmes societies have been created, plays and movies based on the detective have been made, a castle in Switzerland houses a Sherlock Holmes collection, a tavern in London bears his name and features a reconstruction of his rooms in Baker Street. He has even been poked fun at and been called everything from Picklock Holes to Hemlock Jones!

Why such a fuss over a character who appeared in a series of stories close to a century ago? Elementary, dear reader! He is loved. He is loved for his genius, his coolness, his individuality, and for the safety he represents. For as long as Sherlock Holmes is alive the world is somehow safe. The villains will be outsmarted and good and justice will win out. And so he has been kept alive these hundred years by readers around the globe. And since today we are still in need of just such a clever hero it seems a safe deduction that Mr. Sherlock Holmes—and his dear old Watson—will go on living in these pages for a good many more years to come.

The Adventure of the Reigate Puzzle

Another favorite of Conan Doyle, *The Adventure of the Reigate Puzzle,* has had a number of titles over the years. It was originally called *The Adventure of the Reigate Squire,* then it was turned into the plural *The Adventure of the Reigate Squire*s. But when it appeared in the United States it was changed finally to *The Adventure of the Reigate Puzzle.*

The use of handwriting in the story as a means of deducing fact is an interesting device in a mystery. Some experts, however, consider it a shaky one. They believe it impossible to deduce a man's age by his handwriting. But then, Holmes was often capable of the most impossible things.

The Adventure of
the Reigate Puzzle

The spring of 1887 was perhaps the most exhausting time in Sherlock Holmes' life. It was then that he solved a difficult and lengthy mystery. For two months he traveled through Europe working nonstop. It was therefore not surprising when I received a telegram from Europe. It said that Holmes was lying ill in a hotel in France. Within twenty-four hours I was in his sickroom. Luckily, his ailment was not serious. He was simply suffering from the strain of his great work. He seemed nervous and depressed. Thousands of telegrams arrived daily to congratulate him on his success. But they did not cheer him. Nor did the knowledge that he had captured one of the most famed swindlers of all time.

Three days later we were back in Baker Street together. It was clear to me that Holmes needed a change of scenery. My old friend, Colonel Hayter, owned a house in Reigate, Surrey. He had often invited both Holmes and me to visit. The fresh air seemed to me to be just the thing to cure my friend. At first, Holmes did not want to go. But I persuaded him and a week later were under the Colonel's roof.

We sat in the Colonel's gunroom on our first night. Holmes was stretched upon the sofa, while Hayter and I looked over his fine collection of guns.

"By the way," said the Colonel suddenly, "I think I'll

3

take one of these pistols upstairs with me in case we have an alarm."

"An alarm!" said I.

"Yes, we've had a scare around here lately. Old Acton, who lives nearby, had his house broken into last Monday. No damage was done, but the burglars are still loose."

"No clues?" asked Holmes.

"None as yet. But this is just one of our little country crimes. It is too small for your attention, Mr. Holmes. Especially after your great international success."

Holmes waved away the compliment, but his smile showed that it pleased him.

"Was there anything unusual about the break in?" he asked.

"I think not," answered the Colonel. "The thieves ransacked the library. The whole place was turned upside down, but all they got was an old book, two candlesticks, an ivory paperweight, and a ball of twine."

"What an extraordinary assortment!" I exclaimed.

"Oh, the fellows probably grabbed hold of anything they could get," the Colonel responded.

Holmes grunted from the sofa.

"The country police ought to make something of it," said Holmes. "Why it is surely obvious that—"

But I held up a warning finger.

"You are here for a rest, my dear fellow. For heaven's sake, don't get started on a new problem when your nerves are all in shreds."

Holmes shrugged his shoulders like a naughty schoolboy. The talk soon drifted onto other subjects.

But my words of warning were to be wasted. And like it or no, my patient soon became involved in yet another mystery.

We were at breakfast when the Colonel's butler rushed into the dining room.

"Have you heard the news, sir?" he gasped. "At the Cunningham's, sir."

"Burglary!" cried the Colonel.

"Murder!" answered the butler.

The Colonel whistled. "By Jove!" said he. "Who's been killed? Cunningham or his son?"

"Neither, sir. It was William, the coachman. Shot through the heart, sir."

"Who shot him, then?" asked the Colonel.

"The burglar, sir. He was off like a shot and got clean away. William caught him breaking in the door of the pantry. He died trying to protect his master's property."

"What time?"

"It was last night, sir, somewhere about twelve."

"Ah, we'll have to go over to the house," said the Colonel. After the butler had gone, he added, "It's a baddish business. Cunningham is our leading squire around here. He'll be very upset over this. William has worked for him for years. It must have been the same villains who broke into Acton's."

"And stole that odd assortment of objects?" asked Holmes.

"Precisely."

"Hum!" said Holmes. "It may prove to be the simplest matter in the world . . . but it does seem a bit curious, doesn't it? A gang of burglars have broken into two houses right next to one another. Usually burglars vary the location of their crimes, so as not to be discovered by the police. Last night you said that you were going to take a gun upstairs. I remember thinking that this was probably the last area in all England where the burglars would strike again. Which just shows that I still have much to learn."

"I fancy it's some local fellow," said the Colonel. "In that case, Acton's and Cunningham's are just the houses he would strike. They are by far the largest places around."

"And the richest?" asked Holmes.

"Well, they ought to be. But they've been having a legal battle with one another for years. I fancy it has cost them plenty. Old Acton claims that half of Cunningham's estate belongs to him. They have been arguing over it for ages."

"If it's a local villain, there shouldn't be much difficulty catching him," said Holmes, with a yawn. "All right, Watson, don't worry. I don't intend to get involved."

Just then the butler threw open the door.

"Inspector Forrester, sir," he announced.

A smart, eager-looking young fellow stepped into the room.

"Good morning, Colonel," said he. "I hope I'm not intruding. We've heard that Mr. Sherlock Holmes of Baker Street is here."

The Colonel waved his hand toward my friend. The Inspector bowed.

"We thought you might like to aid us in our investigation, Mr. Holmes."

"The Fates are against you, Watson," said Holmes, laughing. "We were chatting about the matter when you came in, Inspector. Perhaps you can let us have the details of the case." Holmes leaned back in his chair to listen. I knew then that my cause was hopeless.

"We had no clue in the Acton affair. But here we have plenty to go on. There's no doubt that it was the same man in each case. He was seen."

"Ah!"

"Yes, sir. But he ran off the instant the shot was fired that killed poor William Kirwan. Mr. Cunningham saw the villain from the bedroom window, and his son, Mr. Alec Cunningham saw him from the back passage. It was a quarter to twelve when they heard William call out. Mr. Cunningham had just got into bed and Mister Alec was smoking a pipe in his dressing room. They both heard the coachman calling for help. Mister Alec ran down the back staircase to see what was the matter. The pantry door was open. As he came to the foot of the stairs he saw two men wrestling outside. One of them fired a shot and the other dropped. Then the murderer rushed across the garden and over a hedge. Mr. Cunningham meanwhile was looking out his bedroom window. He saw the fellow run for the road, but he lost sight of him after that. Mister Alec stopped to see if he could help the dying man and so the villain got clean away. The servants came rushing to see what was the matter. Both Cunninghams said that the burglar was a middle-sized man and was darkly dressed. Beyond that, there are no clues to his appearance. We are making energetic inquiries, however. We hope to find him soon."

"What was this William doing there? Did he say anything before he died?" asked Sherlock Holmes.

"Not a word. He lives with his mother in a nearby cottage. We believe he walked up to the house to make sure all was right. Of course, the Acton burglary has put everyone on their guard. The robber must have just forced open the door when William came upon him."

"Did William say anything to his mother before going out?"

"She is very old and deaf. We can get no information from her. There is one important clue, however. Look at this!"

He took out a small scrap of torn paper and spread it out upon his knee.

"This was found between the finger and thumb of the dead man. It appears to be a part of a larger sheet of paper. You will observe that the hour mentioned is the very time when William met his death. The murderer tore the rest of the page from him. Either that or William took this corner from the murderer. It reads as though it were an appointment."

Holmes took the scrap of paper. It looked like this:

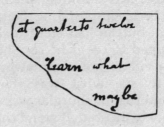

"Suppose this was an appointment," said the Inspector. "It is possible that William was in league with the thief. Perhaps he met the burglar at the house. He may even have helped him break in. Then something happened and they started to fight among themselves."

Holmes was examining the paper closely.

"This writing is of extraordinary interest," said he. "This is a much more serious case than I had thought." He sank his head upon his hands. The Inspector seemed pleased that his little case should interest the famous Sherlock Holmes.

"Your theory is possible," said Holmes. "The burglar and the servant could have been working together. But this writing opens up—" He sank his head into his hands again and remained in the deepest thought for some time. When he raised his face his cheeks were tinged with color. His eyes were as bright as before his illness. He sprang to his feet with his old energy.

"I'll tell you what!" said he. "I should like to have a quiet little glance into the details of this case. There is something in it which fascinates me. If you will permit me, Colonel, I will leave my friend Watson and you. The Inspector and I will go around to the scene of the crime. I want to test the truth of one or two little theories of mine. I will be with you again in half an hour."

An hour and a half passed before the Inspector returned. He was alone.

"Mr. Holmes is walking up and down in the field outside," said he. "He wants us all to go up to the house together."

"To Mr. Cunningham's?" asked the Colonel.

"Yes, sir," he replied.

"What for?"

The Inspector shrugged his shoulders. "I don't quite know, sir. Between ourselves, I think Mr. Holmes has not gotten over his illness yet. He's behaving very queerly, and he is very much excited."

"I don't think you need alarm yourself," said I. "I have usually found that there is method in his madness."

"Some folk might say there is madness in his method," muttered the Inspector. "But he's all on fire to start, Colonel. We best go now."

We found Holmes pacing back and forth outside. His chin was sunk upon his breast and his hands were thrust deep into his trouser pockets.

"The matter grows more interesting," said Sherlock Holmes. "Watson, your country trip has been a distinct success. I have had a charming morning."

"You have been up to the scene of the crime, I understand?" said the Colonel.

"Yes; the Inspector and I have examined the area quite thoroughly."

"Any success?"

"Well, we have seen some very interesting things," Holmes said as we walked on. "First of all, I saw the body of this unfortunate man. He died from a revolver wound as reported."

"Had you doubted it, then?" asked the Colonel.

"Oh, it is good to test everything. We then had an interview with Mr. Cunningham and his son. They were able to point out the exact spot where the murderer jumped over the garden hedge in flight. That was of great interest."

"Naturally."

"Then we had a visit with the poor fellow's mother. We could get no information from her as she is old and feeble."

"And what is the result of your morning's investigation?"

"The belief that the crime is a very peculiar one. Perhaps our visit today will help clear it up. I think we both agree, Inspector, that the scrap of paper found in the dead man's hand is very important. Particularly since it has the exact hour of William's death written on it."

"It should give us a clue, Mr. Holmes."

"It *does* give us a clue. The man who wrote it wanted William Kirwan to be at the house at that time. But why? And where is the rest of that sheet of paper?"

"I examined the ground carefully in the hope of finding it," said the Inspector.

"It was torn out of the dead man's hand," continued Holmes. "Why was someone so anxious to get it? Because it proved his guilt in some way. And what would he do with it? Thrust it into his pocket, most likely. He probably never noticed that a corner of it was missing. We must get the rest of that sheet. Then we shall be close to solving this mystery."

"Yes, but how can we get into the criminal's pocket before we catch the criminal?" asked the Inspector.

"Well, well, it is worth thinking over," answered Holmes. "Then there is another point. The note was sent to William. The man who sent it did not deliver it personally. If he had he would have told William the message. And there would have been no need for a note. So, who brought the note? Or was it mailed to William?"

"I have made inquiries," said the Inspector. "William received a letter yesterday afternoon. The envelope was destroyed by him."

"Excellent!" cried Holmes. He clapped the Inspector on the back. "You've seen the postman! It is a pleasure to work with you. Well, here is William's cottage. Come with me, Colonel, I will show you the scene of the crime."

We passed the pretty cottage where the man had lived. We walked up to the main house. Holmes and the Inspector then led us to the side gate. A policeman was standing at the pantry door.

"Throw the door open, officer," said Holmes. A flight of stairs could now be seen. "It was on those stairs that Mr. Alec Cunningham stood and saw two men struggling just where we are. Old Mr. Cunningham was at that window—the second on the left. He saw the fellow get away over that bush. So did the son. They are both sure of it. Then Mister Alec ran out and knelt beside the wounded man. The ground is very hard and so there are no marks to guide us."

As he spoke two men came down the garden path. One was an elderly man with a strong, deep-lined face. The other was a dashing young fellow. His smiling face and showy dress seemed odd since a tragedy had recently taken place.

"Still at it?" he said to Holmes. "I thought you Londoners were quick."

"Ah! You must give us a little time," said Holmes.

"You'll need some time," said young Alec Cunningham. "Why, I don't see that we have any clues at all."

"There's only one," answered the Inspector. "We thought that if we could find—Good heavens! Mr. Holmes, what is the matter?"

My poor friend's face had suddenly changed color. His eyes rolled upwards and he cringed in agony. Then he groaned and dropped to the ground. We were all horrified. We carried Holmes into the kitchen and placed him in a large chair. He sat there breathing heavily for some minutes. Finally his breathing became more regular. He apologized for his attack and rose from the chair.

"I have only just got over a severe illness," explained Sherlock. "I still suffer from these sudden nervous attacks."

"Shall I send you home in my carriage?" asked old Cunningham.

"Well, since I am here, there is one point I would like to check."

"What is it?" asked Cunningham.

"Well, you all assume that William came on the burglar just as he was breaking in. It is possible that the burglar had already been in the house."

"Why, my son Alec had not yet gone to bed. He certainly would have heard someone moving about," said Old Cunningham.

"Where was he sitting?" asked Holmes.

"I was sitting smoking in my dressing room," answered Alec.

"Which window is that?"

"The last on the left, next to my father's."

"Both your lamps were lit, of course?" asked Holmes.

"Yes."

"There are some very strange points to this case," said Holmes smiling. "Isn't it odd that a professional burglar should break into a house when people are clearly at home and awake?"

"Well, if the case weren't an odd one there wouldn't have been any need to bring you into it in the first place," said the younger man. "As to your idea that the man broke into the house before William tackled him, I think it is absurd. We would have found the place ransacked and missed the things he stole."

"It depends on what things they were," said Holmes. "You must remember that we are dealing with a very peculiar burglar. He seems to work in a particularly strange way. Just look at the odd assortment of things he took from Acton's . . . a ball of string, a paperweight and I don't know what other odds and ends!"

"Well, we are quite in your hands, Mr. Holmes," said old Cunningham. "Anything which you or the Inspector suggest, we will certainly do."

"In the first place," said Holmes, "I should like you to offer a reward. I have written it up for you—if you would just mind signing it. Fifty pounds seems quite enough."

"I would willingly pay five hundred," said Cunningham. Holmes handed him a piece of paper and pencil. "This is not quite correct, however," Cunningham added.

"I wrote it rather hurriedly," answered Holmes.

"You see you begin: 'At a quarter to one on Tuesday morning, an attempt was made—' and so on. It was at a quarter to twelve."

I winced at Holmes' mistake. I knew how such a slip would bother him. He was always very careful about keeping facts straight. It was clear that his recent illness had shaken him badly. This slip was proof that he was far from well. Holmes was clearly embarrassed. The Inspector raised his eyebrows and Alec Cunningham burst into a laugh. The old gentleman corrected the mistake, however, and handed it back to Holmes.

"Get it printed as soon as possible," he said. "I think your idea is an excellent one."

Holmes put the slip of paper carefully into his pocket.

"And now," said he, "let us go through the house and see whether the burglar stole anything."

First, Holmes examined the pantry door. A chisel or strong knife had forced open the lock. We could see the marks in the wood where the lock had been pushed in.

"You don't bar your doors?" asked Holmes.

"We have never found it necessary," answered Mr. Cunningham.

"You don't keep a dog?"

"Yes, but he is chained on the other side of the house."

"When do the servants go to bed?"

"About ten."

"I understand that William was usually in bed at that hour also," said Sherlock.

"Yes."

"It is strange that on this particular night he was up so late," Holmes commented. "Now, I should like you to show us the house, Mr. Cunningham."

The door opened onto a passageway. Off of this passage was the kitchen and a staircase leading to the first floor. It came out onto a landing. Off of this landing was the drawing room and several bedrooms—including those of Mr. Cunningham and his son. Holmes walked slowly around the landing. I could tell by his expression that he was on a hot scent. But I had no idea what it could be.

"My good sir," said Cunningham impatiently. "This is surely unnecessary. That is my room at the end of the stairs, and my son's is the one beyond it. Does it really seem possible that a thief could come up here without disturbing us?"

"I think you are on the wrong track," said the son, with a rather mean smile.

"Still, I must ask you to go along with me a while longer," replied Holmes. "This, I understand, is your son's room"—he pushed open the door—"and that, I presume, is the dressing room where he was smoking when the alarm was given." He stepped across the bedroom, pushed open the door, and glanced around the other chamber.

"I hope you are satisfied now?" said Mr. Cunningham irritably.

"Thank you. I think I have seen all that I wished."

"Then, if it is really necessary we can go into my room."

"If it is not too much trouble," answered Sherlock Holmes.

Cunningham shrugged his shoulders and led the way to his bedroom. We all began to walk toward it. Holmes lagged back until we were the last in the group. Near the foot of the bed there was a small, square table. On it stood a dish of oranges and a bottle of water. As we passed it, Holmes leaned over and knocked the whole thing over on purpose. The glass smashed into a thousand pieces. The fruit rolled into every corner of the room.

"You've done it now, Watson," said he coolly. "A pretty mess you've made of the carpet."

I understood that for some reason Holmes wanted me to take the blame. I stooped down and began to pick up the fruit. The others did the same.

"Hello!" cried the Inspector, "where's he got to?"

Holmes had disappeared.

"Wait here an instant," said young Alec Cunningham. "The fellow is out of his mind. Come with me, Father. We'll see where he's got to."

They rushed out of the room. The Inspector, the Colonel, and I just stood staring at each other in astonishment.

"Pon my word, I am inclined to agree with Mister Alec," said the Inspector. "Perhaps it is because of his illness, but it seems to me that—"

Suddenly there came a scream of "Help! Help! Murder!" It was Holmes' voice. I rushed from the room onto the landing. The cries were coming from the dressing room. I dashed in. The Colonel and the Inspector followed. The two Cunningham's were bending over Sherlock, who was flat on the ground. The younger Cunningham was clutching at his throat with both hands, while the elder seemed to be twisting one of his wrists. In an instant the three of us had torn them off of my friend. Holmes staggered to his feet. He was very pale and seemed exhausted.

"Arrest these men, Inspector!" he gasped.

"On what charge?"

"That of murdering their coachman, William Kirwan!"

The Inspector stared about him in bewilderment. "Oh, come now, Mr. Holmes," he said, "I am sure you don't really mean to—"

"Tut, man; look at their faces!" cried Holmes.

Their guilt was plainly written on their faces. The older man seemed numbed and dazed. He wore a heavy, gloomy expression. His son was no longer a dashing, handsome young man. His eyes were now wild like those of an animal. The Inspector said nothing. He simply raised his whistle to his mouth and blew. Two of his policemen came at once.

"I have no choice but to arrest you, Mr. Cunningham," said he. "I hope that this will prove an absurd mistake. But you can see that—What! Drop it!" Just then, the younger man had taken out a revolver. He was about to cock it. The Inspector had quickly knocked it out of his hand. It clattered to the floor.

Holmes quickly put his foot upon the gun.

"Keep that," he said. "You will find it useful at the trial. But this is what we really wanted." He held up a little crumpled piece of paper.

"The remainder of the note!" cried the Inspector.

"Precisely."

"And where was it?"

"Where I was sure it must be," said Holmes. "I'll make the whole matter clear to you shortly. I think, Colonel, that you and Watson might go home now. I will be along in an hour at the most. The Inspector and I must have a word with the prisoners."

Sherlock Holmes was as good as his word. He was back at the Colonel's house by one o'clock. He had with him a little elderly man. He was introduced as Mr. Acton, whose house had originally been burgled.

"I wanted Mr. Acton to hear my explanation of the case," said Holmes. "I am afraid, Colonel, that you may regret inviting me to stay. I have involved you in quite a drama!"

"On the contrary," answered the Colonel warmly. "I consider it the greatest privilege to have studied your methods of working. However, I must confess that I don't see how you obtained your results!"

"Well, I never hide my methods from a friend—or anyone else who is interested in them. But first I think I shall help myself to a dash of brandy. That struggle in the dressing room shook my nerves!"

"I trust you had no more of your nervous attacks," said the Colonel.

Sherlock Holmes laughed heartily. "We will come to that in its turn," said he. "I will now explain the case to you and show you the points which guided me to my solution. Please interrupt me if anything is not clear.

"There are many skills necessary in detective work. One is to know which are the most important facts of a case. Otherwise, you spend too much time following false leads. In this case, there were two important clues.

"One was revealed in Alec Cunningham's statement. He said that the burglar shot William Kirwan and fled *instantly*. If that was true, then the burglar would not have had time to tear the paper from William's hand. But who else could have done it? Only Alec Cunningham. He was the only person who was with the victim before the servants arrived. The point is a simple one, but the Inspector overlooked it. I therefore suspected Alec Cunningham from the start.

"The second important clue was the scrap of paper itself. I knew that it was of the utmost importance to the case. Here it is. Do you notice anything unusual about it?"

"It is not very neat," said the Colonel.

"My dear sir," cried Holmes. "There can be no doubt. This was written by two persons. They clearly took turns writing every other word. I draw your attention to the strong 't's of 'at' and 'to'. Compare them with the weak ones of 'quarter' and 'twelve'."

"By Jove, two people did write this note! It's as clear as day," said the Colonel. "Why on earth would two men write a letter in such a strange way?"

"Because one of the men did not trust the other and so insisted on splitting all the work equally. Now, it is clear that the man who wrote 'at' and 'to' was the ringleader."

"How can you know that?" asked the Colonel.

"Well, he has the stronger handwriting for one thing. For another, he started the letter and left spaces for the other to fill in. You can see that he did not always leave enough room . . . that is why the second man had to squeeze his 'quarter' in between the 'at' and the 'to'. The man who wrote his words first is clearly the man who planned the affair."

"Excellent!" cried Mr. Acton.

"But not that important," said Holmes. "We now come, however, to a most important point. You may not know it, but experts have been able to tell a man's age from his handwriting. Now in this case it is clear that the stronger handwriting was written by a young man, while the weaker belonged to an older man."

"Excellent!" cried Mr. Acton again.

"There is one other important point here. There is something in common between these handwritings. They belong to men who are blood relatives. Notice the way they both make their 'E's. These are only some of my deductions on observing the scrap of paper. There were twenty-three other deductions. But they would be of more interest to experts than to you. They all made me feel that the Cunninghams, father and son, had written this letter.

"My next step was to examine the details of the crime. I went up to the house with the Inspector. I saw all that was to be seen. I found that the dead man's wound was made at a distance of four yards. If he had been shot at a closer range there would have been gunpowder on his clothes. Alec Cunningham had lied. He had said that the men were struggling when the shot was fired. Also, both father and son had said that the burglar escaped over a hedge. But at that point, there is a broad ditch. The ditch was wet at the bottom. Yet there were no bootmarks near it. I was sure that the Cunninghams had lied about this as well. It was now clear that there had never been a burglar at all.

"And now I had to consider the reason for this crime. I first turned my attention to the burglary at Mr. Acton's. The Colonel told us that there was a lawsuit going on between you, Mr. Acton, and the Cunninghams. I instantly thought that they had broken into your library to find some important papers."

"Precisely so," said Mr. Acton. "There can be no doubt about it. I have the clearest claim on half their present estate. It is all written on a single piece of paper. As it happens, that paper is securely locked away at my lawyer's office. But the Cunninghams did not know that. If they had stolen that paper, my case would have been greatly weakened."

"There you are!" said Holmes, smiling. "It was a dangerous, reckless attempt. It was the type a younger man might have made. They broke in, but found nothing. Then they tried to make it look like an ordinary burglary. They took whatever they could lay their hands on. So far I was clear . . . but there was still much to work out about the case. I needed the rest of the note. I was certain that Alec had torn it out of the dead man's hand. I was almost as certain that he had thrust it into the pocket of his dressing gown. Where else could he have put it? The only question was whether it was still there. It was worth an effort to find out. And that is why I had you all come up to the house with me.

"The Cunninghams joined us outside the pantry door. It was of great importance that they not be reminded of the note. Otherwise, they would have destroyed it immediately. The Inspector was about to tell them of its importance in the case. It was by the luckiest chance that I had my fit at that very moment."

"Good heavens!" cried the Colonel. "Do you mean to say your fit was all an act?"

"Speaking as a medical man, I must say it was well done!" cried I.

"Acting is a most useful art," said Sherlock Holmes. "I then—very cleverly, if I do say so—managed to get old Cunningham to write the word 'twelve'. I did this so that I could compare it with the 'twelve' on the note."

"You wrote a 'quarter to one' on purpose!" I exclaimed. "What an ass I have been!"

"I could see that you felt bad for me," said Holmes. "Sorry about that. We then went upstairs together. We entered the dressing room. I saw the dressing gown hanging on the back of the door. I later upset the table to divert their attention. I then slipped back into the dressing room and examined its pockets. I had just found the note when the Cunninghams came in. I believe they would have murdered me if you hadn't come to my aid. I can still feel the young man's grip at my throat as the father tried to pry open my hand! They saw that I knew all and were desperate.

"I had a little talk with old Cunningham afterward. I wanted to find out exactly why they had committed the crime. He was calm enough although his son was a regular demon. But the father saw that the case against him was strong. He confessed everything. It seems they had searched Mr. Acton's place. William had followed them. He then threatened to blackmail them both. But Mister Alec was a dangerous man to play games with.

He decided to get rid of his blackmailer. He knew that everyone was concerned about more burglaries in the area. And so he decided to hide his crime behind a second one. He lured William to the house with the note. Then he shot him in cold blood."

"But what did the note say?"

Sherlock Holmes placed the note before us. He had taped the two torn pieces together:

> If you will only come round at quarter to twelve to the east gate you will learn what will very much surprise you and maybe be of the greatest service to you and also to Annie Morrison But say nothing to anyone upon the matter

"Of course, we do not know who this Anne Morrison was. But Alec Cunningham knew she was important to William Kirwan.

"The crime was very well thought out," said Holmes. "If they had recovered the note and paid a little more attention to detail, they might have gotten away with it."

"Not with the great Sherlock Holmes upon their trail," said I admiringly.

The
Adventure
of the
Crooked
Man

As one might suspect from the title, *The Adventure of the Crooked Man* is one of Conan Doyle's odder adventures. Its wronged main character, the strange death of the Colonel, the encounter between the crooked man and the Colonel's wife, and the curious creature that is the crooked man's companion, all make for a highly unusual tale. But the adventure lacks one crucial element—Sherlock Holmes' brilliant deductions. Conan Doyle has allowed Holmes to take a backseat in this story. Holmes seeks the help of the crooked man rather than use his own skills of observation and deduction to solve the crime. It is a tribute to Conan Doyle's storytelling that *The Adventure of the Crooked Man* remains an intriguing and popular mystery.

The Adventure of the Crooked Man

"The Adventure of the Crooked Man" took place shortly after my marriage. It began one winter night. My wife had already gone upstairs. I was just about to do the same when I heard the clang of the bell.

I looked up at the clock. It was a quarter to twelve. I wondered what misfortune had brought a patient at so late an hour. I went out into the hall and opened the door. To my astonishment there stood my good friend, Mr. Sherlock Holmes.

"Ah, Watson," said he. "I'd hoped to find you still awake."

"My dear fellow! Come in. Come in!" I said warmly.

"You look surprised to see me. No wonder, it is rather late. I have a favor to ask. Could you put me up tonight?"

"With pleasure," said I.

"Thank you, Watson. Ah, I see you've had a workman in the house. Nothing wrong with the drains, I hope?"

"No, the gas."

"Ah! He has left two nail marks from his boot upon your linoleum. No, thank you. I've had supper. But I'll smoke a pipe with you with pleasure." Holmes seated himself in an armchair near the fire.

I handed him my tobacco pouch. He filled his pipe and smoked it for some time in silence. I could tell that he had a case on his mind, but I waited patiently for him to tell me about it.

"I see you've been rather busy lately," said Holmes at last.

"Yes, I've had a busy day," I answered. "But I don't see how you deduced it."

Holmes chuckled to himself.

"I know your habits, Watson. When you have a great number of patients to see, you take a cab. When the day is slow, you walk. Now, I observe that your boots, while worn, are definitely not dirty. It is only too clear that you took a cab. Therefore, your day was a busy one."

"Excellent!" I cried.

"Elementary," said Holmes. "It is merely a matter of observing clues. Now, at present I am working on one of the strangest cases. Yet I lack the clues to complete my theory. But I'll have them, Watson, I'll have them!" His eyes flashed and color sprang to his usually pale cheeks.

"The problem is most interesting," he continued. "I may say that it is exceptional, in fact. I have already looked into the matter. I believe I have now come within sight of my solution. There is but one step left. I would like you to take that step with me."

"I should be delighted," I said. I liked nothing better than observing Holmes at work.

"Could you travel with me to Aldershot tomorrow morning?" he asked.

"Yes, I can have a friend cover for me here."

"Very good," said Holmes. "I want to get to the station by 11:10."

"That would give me enough time to arrange things."

"Then, if you are not too sleepy, I'll tell you what has happened so far, and what remains to be done."

"I was sleepy before you came, but now I am wide awake!" I exclaimed.

"You may have heard something about the case. It concerns the supposed murder of Colonel Barclay of the Royal Mallows. The facts are only two days old. Briefly, they are these:

"The Royal Mallows is one of the most famous regiments in the British army. Long ago it was stationed in India. But for some years now it has been back in England—at Aldershot. It was commanded up to Monday night by James Barclay. When Barclay was a sergeant he married a Miss Nancy Devoy. She was the daughter of a military man and a favorite of the regiment. It is said that she was a young woman of great beauty. Even now, thirty years later, she is extremely attractive.

"Major Murphy of the Mallows brought me into this case. He has given me most of the facts. According to him, the Barclays' marriage was a happy one. He never heard the couple argue. He did say that Barclay seemed more devoted to his wife than she to him. But they were considered a model couple. There was nothing in their marriage to prepare people for the tragedy to follow.

"The Major said that Barclay was a dashing, jovial

man, although he did have a temper. This side of his personality, however, was never shown to his wife. It also appears that he would sometimes sink into the deepest gloom. He disliked being alone and was afraid of the dark.

"As I said, the Mallows are stationed at Aldershot. The married officers do not live in the barracks. The Colonel and his wife owned a house about a half-mile from camp. It has some grounds, though they border the road. A coachman and two maids work for them. They are the only other people in the house, since the Barclays have no children.

"Mrs. Barclay had a church meeting to go to on Monday evening. It was at 7:30 and so she hurried through dinner. The coachman overheard her chatting with her husband and telling him that she would not be long. She then called on her friend, Miss Morrison, who lives next door. Together they went to their meeting. It lasted forty minutes. At a quarter past nine, Mrs. Barclay dropped off her friend and returned home.

"Now, there is a sun-room at the Barclays'. This room looks out onto the lawn. The lawn is thirty yards deep and is divided from the road by a low wall. On Monday night, Mrs. Barclay returned to this room. The blinds were not drawn as the room is seldom used at night. Mrs. Barclay lit a lamp and rang the bell. She asked the housekeeper to bring her a cup of tea. The Colonel had been sitting in the dining room. When he heard that his wife had returned, he joined her there. The coachman saw him cross the hall and enter the room. James Barclay was never seen alive again.

"The maid was just about to bring in the tea when she heard her master and mistress arguing. She knocked on the door but received no answer. She even turned the handle, but the door was locked from the inside. She ran to tell the cook and they in turn fetched the coachman. The three servants then went into the hall and listened at the door. They all agree that they could hear only two voices—that of the Colonel and his wife. Barclay's voice was low and they could not make out his words. But they could hear his wife. 'You fiend!' she repeated over and over again. 'What can be done now? Give me back my life. I will never so much as breathe the same air with you again!!' Then suddenly there was a dreadful cry from the man and a crash. The woman let out a piercing scream. Again and again she screamed. The coachman rushed at the door and tried to force it open. He was unable to make his way into the room. The maids were too distressed to help him. A sudden thought struck him, however. He ran through the hall door and around to the lawn. One of the sun-room's large windows was open. He climbed into the room. His mistress was now passed out on the sofa. His master's feet were tilted over the side of his armchair. His head was on the ground near the corner of the mantel. He was lying stone dead in a pool of his own blood.

"The coachman saw that he could do nothing for his master. So he tried to open the locked door. But the key was not inside the lock. He couldn't find it anywhere in the room. He had to leave through the open window. He later returned with a policeman and a doctor. They removed Mrs. Barclay to her room. The Colonel's body was then placed on the sofa and a careful examination of the room was made.

"The Colonel's injury was a ragged two-inch long cut at the back of the head. It was caused by a violent blow from a blunt weapon. It was not difficult to guess what that weapon had been. For there, lying beside the body, lay a wooden club. The Colonel collected weapons from foreign lands and so the police assumed this was part of his collection. The servants said that they had never seen it before. It is possible they simply never noticed it. Nothing else of importance was found in the room, on Mrs. Barclay, or on the body of her husband. The door had to be opened by a locksmith.

"On Tuesday morning, Major Murphy called on me and asked for my aid in the investigation. Together we went to Aldershot. My investigations proved to me that the case was even more extraordinary than it first appeared.

"I cross-examined the servants. I did not learn any new facts from them. There was one thing, however, that struck both the servants and the police. That was the look on the dead man's face. The Colonel's face was set in the most dreadful expression of fear and horror. It was so terrible that one person fainted on seeing it. It looked as if the Colonel had seen his own death coming. This agreed with the police's theory. They believe that Barclay watched his wife as she took up the club and struck him. It is true that the blow was struck from behind, but he could have turned his head to dodge the blow. The wife is ill with fever and could not be questioned.

"Her friend, Miss Morrison, was asked if anything had happened during their outing to upset Mrs. Barclay—and turn Mrs. Barclay against her husband. Miss Morrison said no.

"Well, after I gathered these facts, I smoked several pipes and tried to separate the most important facts of the case. Most intriguing was the disappearance of the key. A search had failed to find it. Therefore, it must have been taken from the room. But why? And who could have taken it? Clearly, the Colonel and his wife never left the sun-room. Therefore a third person had to have been there. That third person must have come in through the window. I hoped that a careful examination of the room and the lawn might reveal traces of this mysterious third person.

"You know my methods, Watson. There was not one of them that I did not apply. In the end I did find some footprints ... but very different ones from what I expected. There had indeed been a man in the room. I was able to obtain five very clear impressions of his prints. One was on the road itself. This told me that he had climbed over the low wall. Two were on the lawn, and two were near the window. Actually, he had rushed across the lawn, for his toe-marks were much deeper than his heel-marks. But it was not the man who surprised me. It was his companion."

"His companion!" I exclaimed.

Holmes pulled a large sheet of tissue paper out of his pocket. He carefully unfolded it on his knee.

"What do you make of that?" he asked.

The paper was covered with the tracings of the

footprints of some small animal. It had five well-marked footpads and long nails. The whole print was no bigger than a dessert spoon.

"It's a dog," said I.

"Did you ever hear of a dog running up a curtain? I found distinct traces that this creature had done so."

"A monkey, then?"

"But it is not the print of a monkey."

"What can it be then?" I asked.

"Neither dog, nor cat, nor monkey—nor any creature that we are familiar with. I have tried to reconstruct it from the measurements. Here are four points where the beast stood motionless. You see that it is no less than fifteen inches from forefoot to hindfoot. Add to that the length of the neck and head and you get a creature not much more than two feet long—probably more if there is a tail. But now observe this other measurement. The animal has been moving and we have the length of his stride. In each case it is only three inches. You see, the animal must have a long body with very short legs attached to it. It was not thoughtful enough to leave any hair behind. But I believe its general shape must be as I described. It can run up a curtain and eats meat."

"Eats meat! How do you deduce that?"

"Because it ran up the curtain. A canary's cage was hanging in the window. It seems he was trying to get at the bird."

"Then what was this beast?" I asked.

"Ah, I would be much closer to solving this crime if I

knew that. It is probably some weasel . . . yet it is larger than any I have ever seen."

"But what had it to do with the crime?"

"That is not clear. But we have learned a great deal. We know that a man stood in the road looking at the quarrel between the Barclays. The blinds were up and the lamps were lit. We know also that he ran across the lawn and entered the room with a strange animal. He then either struck the Colonel, or the Colonel fell down from sheer fright at the sight of him, cutting his head on the mantel. Finally, we have the curious fact that the stranger carried off the key."

"Your discoveries seem to make the case even more confusing!" said I.

"Quite so. They show that the affair is much deeper than first suspected. I thought the matter over and have decided to approach the case from a different angle. But really, Watson, I am keeping you up. I can tell you all this tomorrow on the train."

"Thank you, but you've gone too far to stop. Go on, go on," I urged.

"It was quite certain that Mrs. Barclay left the house on good terms with her husband. As I told you, the coachman heard her chatting with the Colonel in a friendly fashion. On her return she went directly to the sun-room . . . a room where she was *least* likely to see her husband. She then ordered tea, which has a soothing effect on the nerves. Obviously, she was upset and needed some time to herself. But her husband did not like being alone. When he heard that she was home, he went directly to her. Mrs. Barclay's anger rose up and she began to argue with him. But why? Something must have happened to her between seven-thirty and nine o'clock—something which caused her to turn on her husband. But what had it been? Miss Morrison had been with her the entire time. She had to know more than she was telling.

"I therefore paid a visit on Miss Morrison. I told her that I was certain she knew the cause of her friend's sudden anger. I assured her that Mrs. Barclay would end up in jail on a murder charge if she did not speak up.

"Miss Morrison is a little slip of a girl, with timid eyes and blond hair. She sat thinking for some time after I had spoken. Then she turned to me.

" 'I promised my friend that I would say nothing of the matter. A promise is a promise. But I had no idea there was so serious a charge against her. If I can help her by speaking the truth, especially when her lips are sealed by illness, then I shall. I am sure she would no longer hold me to my promise. I will tell you exactly what happened on Monday evening.

" 'We were returning from the Mission at about a quarter to nine. On our way we had to pass through Hudson Street. There is only one lamp on the left-hand side of the street. As we approached the lamp, I saw a man come toward us. His back was very crooked. Something like a box was slung over one of his shoulders. He carried his head low and walked with his knees bent. We were passing him when he raised his face and looked at us. Suddenly he stopped and screamed out in a dreadful voice, "My God, it's Nancy!" Mrs. Barclay turned white as death. She would have fallen down had he not caught her. I was going to call for the police, but to my surprise she spoke to him in a friendly way.

" ' "I thought you had been dead these thirty years, Henry," said she. Her voice shook.

" ' "So I have," said he. He looked both bitter and sad. His hair and whiskers were shot with gray and his face was all crinkled and puckered like a withered apple.

" ' "Just walk on a little way, dear," said Mrs. Barclay to me. "I want to have a word with this man. There is nothing to be afraid of." She tried to speak boldly, but she was still deadly pale. She could hardly get the words out of her trembling lips.

" 'I did as she asked me and they talked for a few minutes. Then she came down the street toward me. Her eyes were afire. I could see the crooked man standing by the lamppost. He was shaking his clenched fists, as if he were mad with rage. She never said a word until we were at this door. Then she took me by the hand and begged me not to tell anyone what had happened. When I promised, she kissed me. I have not seen her since. I have told you the whole truth.'

"That was her statement, Watson. It was a light in the dark to me. Suddenly the pieces of the puzzle began to fit together. I now had to find that crooked man. I spent much of the day in search of him. By evening—this very evening, Watson—I ran him down. The man's name is Henry Wood. He lives in rented rooms right in Hudson Street where the ladies met him. He has only been there five days. The landlady told me that he is a magician and performer. He performs nightly at the regiment canteen. He carries some creature in that box.

She seemed quite afraid of the animal and said she had never seen one like it before. It seems he uses it in some of his tricks. She also mentioned that he sometimes spoke in a strange language and that for the last two nights she has heard him groaning and weeping in his bedroom. She said that he paid his bill on time, but once had given her a bad coin. She showed it to me, Watson. It was an Indian rupee.

"So now, my dear fellow, you know all the facts. It is perfectly plain that after their meeting, he followed Nancy Devoy. He saw the quarrel between husband and wife through the window, and rushed in. The creature he carried in his box got loose. But what happened next? He is the only person in this world who can tell us exactly what happened in that room."

"And you intend to ask him?"

"Most certainly—but in the presence of a witness," said Holmes.

"And am I the witness?"

"Yes," he answered. "If he can clear the matter up, well and good. But if he refuses, we may have to get a warrant and arrest him."

"But how do you know he will be there when we return?"

"You may be sure of that. I have one of my Baker Street boys standing guard. The boy will follow him wherever he goes. We shall find him in Hudson Street tomorrow, Watson, mark my words. Meanwhile I shall be a criminal myself if I keep you from your bed any longer!"

* * *

We were in Aldershot by midday. We made our way at once to Hudson Street. I could see that Holmes was excited—I, too, felt a quickness of heart as we neared the crooked man's rooms. There was nothing quite like being with Holmes on the trail of a mystery.

"This is the street," said he. "Ah! Here is my guard, Simpson."

"He's up there, Mr. Holmes," cried a scruffy-looking lad.

"Good, Simpson," said Holmes, patting him on the head. "Come along, Watson. This is the house." A moment later we were in the crooked man's room. A fire was blazing and the room was like an oven. The man was crouching over the fire. He turned his face toward us as we entered. It was worn and weathered. Still, I could see that it had once been handsome. He did not rise, but waved toward two chairs.

"Mr. Henry Wood, late of India, I believe?" said Sherlock Holmes. "I've come over this little matter of Colonel Barclay's death."

"What should I know about it?" the man asked gruffly.

"That's what I want to find out. I know that Mrs. Barclay is an old friend of yours. Unless the matter is cleared up, she will probably be tried for murder."

The man gave a violent start.

"I don't know who you are," he cried, "nor how you come to know what you do. Will you swear that this is true?"

"Why, they are only waiting for the fever to pass before they arrest her."

"My God! Are you in the police yourself?"

"No."

"What business is it of yours, then?"

"It's every man's business to see justice done," Sherlock Holmes answered.

"You can take my word that she is innocent," the crooked man replied.

"Then you are guilty?"

"No, I am not."

"Who killed Colonel James Barclay then?"

"It was Fate that killed him. Mind you, I had it in my heart to kill him, and he would have had what was coming to him. And I might have killed him, had his guilty conscience not done it first. You want me to tell the story. Well, I don't know why I shouldn't.

"It was this way, sir. You see me now with my back like a camel and my ribs out of place. But there was a time when Corporal Henry Wood was the handsomest man in the Royal Mallows. We were in India then. Barclay was the sergeant in my company and Nancy Devoy was the finest girl that ever lived. There were two men who loved her and one whom she loved. And you'll smile when you look at this poor thing huddled before the fire, and hear me say that it was for my good looks that she loved me.

"Well, I had her heart, but her father was set on her marrying Barclay. I was a poor, reckless young man, while Barclay had an education and future. The girl held true to me and it seemed that she would marry me. But then, the country was turned upside down.

"Civil War broke out and the Indian people revolted

against the British presence in their country. Ten thousand rebels surrounded our regiment. We were trapped—soldiers, women, children. After two weeks our water began to run out. We had no contact with the outside world. Our only hope was to somehow send a message to General Neill. Neill was in charge of the British Army in India and could send troops to our rescue. I volunteered to tell General Neill of our danger. My offer was accepted. I talked it over with Sergeant Barclay. He was supposed to know the area better than anyone else in the troop. He drew me up a route to guide me through rebel lines. At ten o'clock the same night I started off upon my journey. There were a thousand lives to save, but I could think only of one.

"I dropped over the wall and made my way along a dried-up watercourse. We had hoped it would screen me from the enemy's lookouts. I crept along it. An instant later I was stunned by a blow. Six rebels had been waiting for me in the dark. They bound me hand and foot. But the real blow was to my heart. As I came to and listened to them, I understood that it had been a trap. Barclay had betrayed me. He had given me the wrong route so that he could claim Nancy as his own.

"Well, there's no need for me to dwell on that part of the story. You know now what James Barclay was capable of. General Neill had learned of our plight from another source and rescued our regiment the very next day. But the rebels took me away with them. I was tortured. Each time I tried to escape, I was captured and tortured again. It was many years before I could flee. But by then what was the use? What use was it for me, a

wretched cripple, to go back to England, or make myself known to my old comrades? Even my wish for revenge would not make me do that. I preferred for Nancy and my old pals to think of Henry Wood as having died with a straight back than to see him living and crawling like a chimpanzee. They never doubted that I was dead and I never meant that they should. I heard that Barclay had married Nancy and that he had been promoted in the regiment, but even that did not make me speak.

"But when one gets old, one has a longing for home. For years I've been dreaming of the bright green fields and hedges of England. At last I decided to see them before I died. I saved enough to bring me across and I came here, where the soldiers are. I know the soldiers' ways and how to amuse them and so can earn enough money to live."

"Your story is most interesting," said Sherlock Holmes. "I have already heard of your meeting with Mrs. Barclay. You then, I understand, followed her home and witnessed an argument between her husband and herself. It was doubtless over his despicable treatment of you. Your own feelings overcame you and you ran across the lawn and broke in upon them."

"I did, sir, and at the sight of me his entire body tensed and changed color. He went head over heels over his chair and banged his head against the mantel. But he was dead before he fell. I read death on his face as plain as day. The sight of me was like a bullet through his guilty heart."

"And then?"

"Then Nancy fainted. I took the key from her hand to unlock the door and get help. But it suddenly seemed better to leave it alone. The Colonel's death could easily look like murder. And I certainly had a motive. So I thrust the key into my pocket. Teddy had run up the curtain and I dropped my stick while I was chasing him. I got him back into his box and was off as fast as I could run."

"Who's Teddy?" asked Holmes and I at once.

The man leaned over and pulled up the front of a small hutch. Out slipped a beautiful reddish-brown creature, with a long thin nose and the finest red eyes that I ever saw in an animal's head.

"It's a mongoose!" I cried.

"Well, some call them that, and some call them ichneumon," said the man. "Snakecatcher is what I call them. Teddy is amazing quick catching cobras. I have one here without fangs and Teddy catches it every night to please the folks in the canteen. Any other point, sir?"

"Well, we may have to visit you again, if Mrs. Barclay should prove to be in serious trouble."

"In that case, of course, I'll come forward."

"But if not, there's no point in raking up this scandal against a dead man—even if he did act in the cruelest, foulest way. At least you have the satisfaction of knowing that he lived with a guilty conscience for thirty years. And it is quite likely that it killed him in the end. Ah, there goes Major Murphy on the other side of the street. Goodbye, Wood, I want to learn if anything has happened since yesterday." We left the crooked man in front of his fire and overtook Murphy at the corner.

"Ah, Holmes," he said. "I suppose you have heard that all this fuss has come to nothing."

"What then?" Sherlock Holmes asked.

"The medical evidence shows that Barclay's death was from natural causes, probably shock of some kind. I'm sorry to have wasted your valuable time. It seems the case was quite ordinary after all."

The Adventure of the Greek Interpreter

The Adventure of the Greek Interpreter introduces us to a new and delightful character in the Sherlock Holmes adventures—Holmes' older brother. Mycroft Holmes is everything we would expect in a brother of Sherlock—and more! He's just as smart, even more eccentric, and twice Holmes' size. . . . Together Mycroft and Sherlock make quite a pair!

The men's club that Mycroft helped found was not unusual in the late 1800's in London. Such clubs, which catered to members' tastes, were common. There were clubs for actors, politicians, game players, gamblers, hunters. There are still clubs to be found in London, but most admit women and few, if any, are quite as unsociable as the one described here!

The Adventure of the Greek Interpreter

I had never heard Mr. Sherlock Holmes speak of his family. In fact, I had come to believe that he was an orphan. I was therefore surprised when one day he began to talk to me about his brother.

I remember it was after tea on a summer evening. We were talking about whether a person is born with certain talents or whether they are acquired through education.

"In your own case," said I, "it seems clear that your skills in observation and deduction are due to your own studies."

"To some extent," said Sherlock Holmes. "My ancestors were country squires. They lived the quiet life. They certainly did not go about solving crimes! Still, I believe my skills as a detective are in the blood."

"But how do you know that?" I asked.

"Because my brother, Mycroft, is also talented that way. In fact, his skills are superior to mine."

This was news to me indeed! Could there be another man in England with such a genius for deduction? And if so, why hadn't the police or the public heard of him? I hinted to Sherlock that it was his own modesty which made him say that his brother was his superior. Holmes laughed at the suggestion.

"My dear Watson," said he. "Modesty is a foolish

trait. To the man who uses his mind—who reasons logically—all things should be seen exactly as they are. When I say that Mycroft has better powers than I, you may take it that I am speaking the exact truth."

"Is he your junior?" I asked.

"No. He is seven years my senior."

"Why is he unknown?"

"Oh, he is very well known in his own circle," Sherlock answered.

"Where, then?" asked I.

"Well, at the Diogenes Club, for example."

I had never heard of it. My face must have said so, for Holmes pulled out his watch.

"The Diogenes Club is the queerest club in London. And Mycroft is one of its queerest members. He's always there from a quarter to five till twenty to eight. It's six now, so if you care for a stroll, I shall be happy to introduce you to both."

Five minutes later we were in the street on our way to the Diogenes Club.

"You wonder," said my friend, "why it is that Mycroft does not use his powers for detective work. He is incapable of it."

"But I thought you said—!"

"I said that he was my superior in observation and deduction. If the art of the detective could be performed from an armchair, then my brother would be the greatest detective that ever lived. But he has no ambition and no energy. He will not even go out of his way to learn if his deductions are correct. He would rather be considered wrong than take the trouble to prove himself right. Again and again I have taken a problem to him. Each time I have received an explanation that proved correct. And yet he would not work out the practical points necessary for a case to be brought to trial."

"It is not his profession, then?"

"Not at all. What is to me a means of livelihood is to him a mere hobby. He has an extraordinary mind for numbers and works for the government. Mycroft lives near the club and the government buildings. In the morning he walks around the corner to work and in the evening he walks back around again. From year's end to year's end he takes no other form of exercise. He is seen nowhere except at the Diogenes Club and work."

"I have never heard of the club," said I.

"Very likely not. There are many men in London who do not care for the company of others. Yet they are not in the least against comfortable chairs and the latest magazines. The Diogenes Club was started for this type of man. It now contains some of the most unsociable men in town. No member is permitted to take the least notice of anyone else. No talking is permitted except in the Stranger's Room. If one of the members is caught talking three times, he may be expelled from the club. My brother was one of the founders. At times, I myself have found it a very soothing place."

We had now reached the door of this strange men's club. Holmes motioned for me not to speak and led me into the hall. Through the glass paneling I could see a large and luxurious room beyond. Many men were reading papers, each sitting in his own little nook. Holmes showed me into the Stranger's Room and left. In a minute he came back with a companion. I knew this man could only be Sherlock's brother.

Mycroft Holmes was much larger and fatter than Sherlock. His body was very round, but his face had something of Sherlock's sharpness. His eyes were a light watery gray and seemed always to have a faraway look. It was a look that I had seen in Sherlock's eyes only when he was in the deepest thought.

"I am glad to meet you, sir," said Mycroft Holmes. He put a broad, fat hand out to shake. It was like the flipper of a seal. "Your writings have made my brother quite famous. I hear about him everywhere. By the way, Sherlock, I expected to see you last week. I thought you'd consult me over that Manor House case. I thought you might be a little out of your depth."

"No, I solved it," said my friend, smiling.

"It was Adams, of course?"

"Yes, it was Adams."

"I was sure of it from the start," said Mycroft Holmes. The two brothers sat down together in the bow window. "This is the perfect spot to study mankind!" said Mycroft. "Look at the magnificent types walking by! Look at these two men coming toward us, for example."

"The candle-maker and the other?" asked Holmes.

"Precisely. What do you make of the other?"

The two men had stopped opposite the window. Some wax stains over one of the men's pockets were the only signs of candles I could see. The other was a very small fellow. He was darkly dressed and carried several packages under his arm.

"An old soldier, I perceive," said Sherlock.

"And very recently discharged," remarked the brother.

"Served in India, I see."

"An officer, no doubt . . . and a widower," added Mycroft.

"But with a child," said Sherlock.

"Children, my dear boy, children."

"Come," said I, laughing. "This is a little too much."

"The man has the bearing and expression of authority," said Sherlock. "He is clearly a soldier with rank. His sunburned skin shows that he was recently in India."

"Yes, he was recently discharged from the army. He is still wearing his army or 'ammunition boots' as they are called," observed Mycroft. "Then, of course, his complete mourning shows that he has lost someone very dear. He is doing the shopping, so we can assume that it was his wife. He has been buying things for children. There is a rattle, which shows that one of them is very young. He has a picture book under his arm. This shows that there is a second child to think of."

Sherlock had said that Mycroft possessed superior deductive talents. I was beginning to see what he meant.

"By the way, Sherlock," said he. "A rather interesting case has come my way. You might like following it through. I really don't have the energy to do it. I have enjoyed mulling the problem over, though. If you would care to hear the facts —"

"My dear Mycroft, I should be delighted," said Holmes.

The brother scribbled a note upon a piece of paper. He then rang the bell and handed the note to the waiter when he came.

"I have asked Mr. Melas to step in," said he. "He

lives in my building. Mr. Melas is Greek. He earns his living as an interpreter. I will leave it to him to tell you of his remarkable experience."

A few minutes later we were joined by Mr. Melas. He was a short, stout man. His olive skin and black hair showed that he was from the south, but he spoke perfect English. He shook hands eagerly with Sherlock Holmes.

"I do not think the police believe my story," said he. "I will not rest until I know what happened to that poor man with bandages all over his face!"

"I am all attention!" exclaimed Sherlock Holmes.

"This is Wednesday evening," said Mr. Melas. "Well, it all happened on Monday night—two days ago. I am an interpreter. In fact, for many years I have been the chief Greek interpreter in London. My services are used by all sorts of people. I translate for diplomats, for tourists, for businessmen . . . .

"Strangers who do not speak English often run into difficulties. It is not unusual for me to be sent for at odd hours. I was therefore not surprised on Monday night when a Mr. Latimer came to my rooms. He was a very fashionably dressed young man. He said that a Greek friend had come to see him on business. This friend did not speak English well and Mr. Latimer did not speak Greek. Clearly they needed the services of an interpreter. He said that his house was a little ways away in Kensington. He wanted me to come with him at once. He had a cab waiting and he bustled me into it as soon as we were in the street.

"I say that it was a cab. But it was actually more like a private carriage. It was certainly more roomy and plush than the usual cab. Mr. Latimer seated himself opposite me. He said little and so I stared out the window. I soon realized that we were going out of our way. I mentioned this to him. My words were immediately stopped by his extraordinary conduct.

"He drew out from his pocket a rather mean-looking club. He shifted it back and forth between his hands. Then he placed it upon the seat beside him. Next he drew up the windows. They were covered with paper so that I could not see out!

" 'I am sorry to cut off your view, Mr. Melas,' said he. 'The fact is that I do not want you to know where we are going. It might prove inconvenient for me if you could find your way there again.'

"I was utterly taken aback by his words. My companion was a powerful, broad-shouldered young man. Even without his weapon, I would not stand a chance in a struggle.

" 'This is very extraordinary conduct, Mr. Latimer,' I stammered. 'You must be aware that what you are doing is illegal.'

" 'We'll make it up to you,' said he. 'But I warn you, you will be in serious trouble if you try to raise an alarm. I beg you to remember that no one knows where you are. Whether you are in this carriage, or in my house, you are totally within my power.' He spoke softly, but there was menace in his words.

"I sat in silence, wondering what on earth could be his reason for kidnapping me.

"We drove for nearly two hours. I hadn't the least clue where we were going. It was a quarter past seven when we left my rooms. It was ten minutes to nine when we at last came to a standstill. My companion lowered the window. I caught a glimpse of a low, arched doorway with a burning lamp above it. I was hurried from the carriage. The door was flung open and I found myself inside.

"The room was dark and I could see little. In the dim light I could just see the person who had opened the door. He was a small, mean-looking, middle-aged man with rounded shoulders. As he turned toward us I saw that he was wearing glasses.

" 'Is this Mr. Melas, Harold?' the man asked.

" 'Yes,' replied my kidnapper.

" 'Well done! Well done! No ill-will, Mr. Melas, I hope. We could not get on without you. If you deal fair with us, you'll not regret it. But if you try any tricks, God help you!'

"He spoke in a jerky, nervous fashion, and giggled in-between his words. But there was nothing funny about him. In fact, he filled me with fear.

" 'What do you want with me?' I asked.

" 'There is a Greek gentleman visiting us. He does not speak English. We wish you simply to ask him a few questions. But say more than you are told to and you'll wish you were never born!'

"As he spoke he opened a door and led me into the room beyond. This room too was dimly lit. There was a chair under the lamp and the man motioned for me to sit in it. Latimer had left, but he now returned with a gentleman. I was filled with horror on seeing this man. He was deathly pale and terribly thin. But what shocked me was the sight of his face. It was crisscrossed with bandages! A large one was fastened over his mouth.

" 'Have you the slate, Harold?' cried the older man. 'Are his hands loose? Now then, give him the pencil. You are to ask the questions, Mr. Melas. He will write the answers. Ask him whether he is prepared to sign the papers.'

"I asked the question. The man's eyes flashed fire.

" 'Never,' he wrote in Greek on the slate.

" 'On no conditions?' I asked at the request of our tyrant.

" 'Only if I see her married by a Greek priest whom I know.'

"The older man giggled in his evil way.

" 'You know what awaits you then?' he asked.

" 'I care nothing for myself,' the Greek answered.

"These are samples of the questions and answers which made up our strange half-written, half-spoken conversation. Again and again I had the same reply. But soon a happy thought came to me. I took to adding little sentences of my own to each question. At first they were innocent ones—meant to see whether our companions understood what I was doing. When it was clear that they did not, I begun to play a more dangerous game. Our conversation ran something like this:

" 'You can do no good by refusing. *Who are you?*'

" 'I care not. *I am a stranger in London.*'

" 'Your fate will be on your own head. *How long have you been here?*'

" 'Let it be so. *Three weeks.*'

" 'The property can never be yours. *What ails you?'*

" 'It shall not go to villains. *They are starving me.'*

" 'You shall go free if you sign. *What house is this?'*

" 'I will never sign. *I do not know.'*

" 'You are not doing her any service. *What is your name?'*

" 'Let me hear her say so. *Kratides.'*

" 'You shall see her if you sign. *Where are you from?'*

" 'Then I shall never see her. *Athens.'*

"Another five minutes, Mr. Holmes, and I should have wormed out the whole story right from under their noses. My next question might have cleared the matter up. But at that instant the door opened. A woman stepped into the room. I could not see her well, but she was tall and graceful. She had black hair and was dressed in a sort of loose, white gown.

" 'Harold!' said she. She spoke English with a broken accent. 'I could not stay away longer. It is so lonely up there with only—oh, my God, it is Paul!'

"These last words were in Greek. At the same instant the man tore the bandage from his lips. He screamed, 'Sophy! Sophy!' and rushed into the woman's arms. Their embrace was but an instant. Latimer seized the woman and pushed her out of the room. Meanwhile the older man easily overpowered his weak victim and dragged him from the room. For a moment I was left alone. I sprang to my feet in search of a clue to tell me where we were. Fortunately I took no steps. The older man had returned and his eyes were fixed on me.

" 'That will do, Mr. Melas,' said he. 'You see that we have taken you into our confidence. This business is of a very private nature. Here is your fee. Now remember—do not speak to anyone about this. If you do, well, God have mercy on your soul!'

"This man filled me with loathing and horror. The lamp now shone on him and I could see him better. His features were dark and his little pointed beard was thin. He pushed his face forward as he spoke and his lips and eyes were always twitching.

" 'We shall know if you speak of this to anyone,' said he. 'We have our own means of finding things out. Now you will find the carriage waiting. My friend will see you on your way.'

"I was hurried into the carriage. Mr. Latimer followed close at my heels. He took his place opposite me. We drove in silence. It was after midnight when the carriage came to a stop.

" 'You will get out here, Mr. Melas,' said Latimer. 'I am sorry to leave you so far from your house. But I have no choice. Any attempt to follow this carriage will lead to injury to yourself.'

"He opened the door as he spoke. I hardly had time to spring out before the coachman lashed the horse and the carriage rattled away. I looked around me in astonishment. I stood wondering where on earth I might be. Luckily a man was walking toward me. He was a railway porter.

" 'Can you tell me what place this is?' I asked.

" 'Wandsworth Common,' said he.

" 'Can I get a train into town?'

" 'If you walk a mile or so you'll come to the station,' he said. 'You'll just be in time for the last train to London.'

"So that was the end of my adventure, Mr. Holmes. I do not know where I was or who these villains were. But I know there is foul play going on! I want to help that unhappy man if I can. The next morning I told the whole story to Mr. Mycroft Holmes and then to the police."

We all sat in silence for some time after listening to this extraordinary story. Then Sherlock Holmes looked across at his brother.

"Have you taken any steps?" he asked.

Mycroft picked up the *Daily News* which lay nearby. He read the following:

"REWARD FOR INFORMATION ABOUT A GREEK GENTLEMAN NAMED PAUL KRATIDES. HE IS FROM ATHENS AND DOES NOT SPEAK ENGLISH. A SIMILAR REWARD WILL BE PAID TO ANYONE GIVING INFORMATION ABOUT A GREEK LADY WHOSE FIRST NAME IS SOPHY.

That was in all the daily papers. I've had no answers yet."

"How about the Greek Embassy?" Sherlock asked.

"I have inquired. They know nothing."

"A wire to the head of the Athens police, then . . ."

"Sherlock has all the ambition in the family," said Mycroft to me. "Well, you take on the case. Let me know if you find anything out."

"Certainly," answered my friend. He rose from his chair. "I'll let you and Mr. Melas know anything that turns up. In the meantime, Mr. Melas, I should be on my guard if I were you. Now that this advertisement has appeared in the papers, these villains must know that you have betrayed them."

On the way home, Holmes stopped at a telegraph office and sent off several wires.

"You see, Watson," he remarked, "our evening has not been wasted. Some of my most interesting cases have come to me through Mycroft. The problem we have just listened to presents some interesting features."

"You have hopes of solving it?" I asked.

"Well, we know quite a bit already. I think it would be very unusual for us not to discover the rest. You must have formed some theory to explain the facts."

"In a vague way, yes," I answered.

"What was your idea then?"

"It seemed to me that this Greek girl was carried off by the young Englishman named Harold Latimer."

"Carried off from where?" Holmes asked.

"Athens, perhaps."

Sherlock Holmes shook his head. "This young man could not talk a word of Greek. The lady could speak English fairly well. She must have been in England some time, but he has not been in Greece."

"Well then, she came on a visit to England, and Harold persuaded her to elope with him."

"That is more likely."

"Then the brother—that I fancy is the relationship—comes over to interfere. The young man and his older friend seize him. They use violence to try to make him sign over the girl's fortune to them. This he refuses to do. To deal with him they have to have an interpreter.

So they find Mr. Melas. The girl is not told of her brother's arrival and finds out by the merest accident."

"Excellent, Watson," cried Holmes. "I really fancy that you are not far from the truth. You see we know all the facts. We only have to fear some act of violence on their part. If they give us time, we'll catch them."

"But how can we find their house?" I asked.

"We must hope to trace this girl, Sophy Kratides. Clearly the brother is a complete stranger. But he had time to hear of his sister's plight and travel here from Greece. She must therefore have been in England at least some weeks. Hopefully, she's been living in the same place all this time. If she has, there's a good chance someone will know her and respond to Mycroft's advertisement."

We had reached Baker Street by this time. Holmes walked up the stairs in front of me. As he opened the door of the room he gave a start of surprise. Sitting in the armchair was his brother Mycroft.

"Come in, Sherlock! Come in, sir," said he. He smiled at our surprised faces. "You don't expect such effort from me, do you, Sherlock? But somehow this case attracts me."

"How did you get here?" Sherlock asked.

"I passed you in a cab."

"Has there been some new development?"

"I had an answer to my advertisement."

"Ah!"

"Yes; it came a few minutes after you left."

"And what did it say?" asked Sherlock.

Mycroft Holmes took out a sheet of paper.

"Here it is," said he, "written by a size J fountain pen on royal cream paper by a middle-aged man:

SIR:
I KNOW THE YOUNG LADY SOPHY VERY WELL. IF YOU CALL ON ME, I CAN TELL YOU OF HER PAINFUL HISTORY. SHE IS LIVING AT PRESENT AT THE MYRTLES, BECKENHAM. YOURS, FAITHFULLY,
                              J. DAVENPORT

"He gives his address," said Mycroft Holmes. "Don't you think we should drive out to him and learn her story?"

"My dear Mycroft, the brother's life is more valuable than the sister's story. I think we should call at Scotland Yard for Inspector Gregson and a search warrant. Then we will go straight to Beckenham. A man is being tortured. Every moment is precious."

"Better pick up Mr. Melas on our way," I suggested. "We may need an interpreter."

"Excellent!" said Sherlock Holmes. "Send the boy for a cab and we'll be off at once." He opened the table drawer as he spoke. I noticed that he slipped his revolver into his pocket. "Yes," said he, in answer to my glance. "We seem to be dealing with a dangerous gang."

It was almost dark before we reached Mr. Melas' rooms. A gentleman had just called for him and he was gone.

"Can you tell me where they went?" asked Mycroft Holmes.

"I don't know, sir," answered the woman who had

opened the door. "I only know that he drove away with the gentleman in a carriage."

"Did the gentleman give a name?"

"No, sir."

"Was he a tall, handsome, dark young man?"

"Oh, no, sir. He was a little gentleman with glasses. He was very thin and seemed pleasant. He was laughing all the time he was talking!"

"Come along!" cried Sherlock Holmes. "This grows serious! These men have got hold of Melas again. No doubt they need his professional services. But they may try to punish him for speaking out."

We intended to take a train to Beckenham. We hoped to reach the house before or soon after the carriage. But it took us more than an hour to find Inspector Gregson and get a search warrant at Scotland Yard. It was half past ten before we arrived at Beckenham. A drive of half a mile took us to the Myrtles. It was a large, dark house standing back from the road. We dismissed our cab and made our way up the drive on foot.

"The windows are all dark," remarked the Inspector. "The house seems deserted."

"Our birds have flown and the nest is empty," said Holmes.

"Why do you say so?" asked the Inspector.

"A carriage heavily loaded with luggage departed during the last hour."

The Inspector laughed. "Yes, Holmes, I, too, saw the wheel tracks by the light of the gatelamp. But how do you know it was loaded with luggage?"

"There are two sets of wheel tracks. One coming in

and one going out," answered Sherlock Holmes. "The outbound ones are very much deeper—so much so that we can safely say that a considerable weight had been placed in the carriage."

The Inspector shook his head. "You are most observant," he said. "The front door will not be easy to force open. But if no one answers, we'll have to try it." He hammered loudly at the knocker and pulled at the bell. No one responded. Holmes had slipped away, but he came back in a few minutes.

"I have a window open," said he.

"It is a good thing that you are on the side of the law and not against it, Mr. Holmes!" remarked the Inspector. "Well, under the circumstances, I think we may enter without waiting for an invitation."

One after the other we made our way into a large room. The Inspector lit his lantern. By its light we could see the table. On it lay two glasses, an empty brandy bottle, and the remains of a meal.

"What is that?" asked Holmes suddenly.

We all stood still and listened. A low moaning sound was coming from somewhere above our heads. Holmes rushed to the door and out into the hall. The noise was coming from upstairs. He dashed up with the Inspector and me at his heels. His brother Mycroft followed as quickly as his bulk would permit.

Three doors faced us on the second floor. A haunting, eerie sound came from the center one. The door was locked but the key was on the outside. Holmes flung it open and rushed in. A moment later he was out again. His hand clutched at his throat.

"It's charcoal," he cried. "The fumes are poisonous. Give it time to clear."

We peered into the room. The only light came from a dull, blue flame which flickered from a small hanging burner. It threw an unnatural circle of light upon the floor. Two vague figures crouched against the wall. The fumes were so strong that even at the door we coughed and gasped for air. Holmes took a deep breath and dashed into the room. He threw the window open and the coalburner out into the garden below. Then he darted out again.

"We can enter in a minute," he gasped. "Where is a candle? I doubt if we could strike a match in that atmosphere. The room would probably blow up. Hold the light at the door and we shall get them out, Mycroft. Now!"

With a rush we got to the poisoned men and dragged them out onto the landing. Both of them were blue-lipped and insensible. Their faces were swollen and their eyes were bulging. The Greek interpreter's hands and feet were securely strapped together. Over one eye was the mark of a violent blow. The other man was tied in a similar fashion. He was frighteningly thin. Bandages were taped all over his face in the most bizarre design. He had ceased to moan as we laid him down. A glance showed me that we had come too late to save him. Mr. Melas, however, still lived.

In an hour he was able to tell us what had happened. It seemed that Latimer had come to his rooms with a revolver and had kidnapped him a second time. He had been taken to Beckenham and forced to act as an interpreter during a second interview. That interview was even more dramatic than the first. The two Englishman had threatened Kratides with death if he did not agree to their demands. But he would not give in. Finally they had hurled him back into his prison. Then they had accused Melas of betraying them. They had seen the advertisement in the papers. In their rage, they had struck him over the eye with a stick. He remembered nothing more until he found us bending over him.

We were able to learn about Sophy and Paul Kratides from J. Davenport—the man who answered the advertisement. It seemed that Sophy Kratides came from a wealthy Greek family. She had come to England to visit some friends. While there she had met a young man named Harold Latimer. He had gained influence over her and had persuaded her to elope with him. Her friends were shocked at the event and had contacted her brother in Athens. The brother had arrived in England and had found Latimer and his associate—Wilson Kemp. But then the tables had turned. These two villains had seized him and kept him prisoner. They had tried through cruelty and starvation to make him sign away his own and his sister's property. They had kept him in the house without the girl's knowledge. The bandages on the face were to disguise him, in case she saw him. But she had instantly seen through the disguise during the interpreter's first visit. But by then the poor girl was herself a prisoner. Finally they realized that her brother would not sign the papers. They placed him and the interpreter in the poisoned room. Then they fled with the girl.

Months afterward we read about a curious incident

in Budapest. The paper told of two Englishmen who had been traveling with a woman. The men had been stabbed to death. The Hungarian police were of the opinion that they had quarreled and killed each other in the fight.

"Nonsense," said Holmes on reading the article. "The girl, Sophy, holds the key to this mystery. Find her and you will learn how she and her brother were avenged."

Mycroft Holmes agreed wholeheartedly. Despite the tragic ending of "The Adventure of the Greek Interpreter" there were many mysteries to come in which Sherlock Holmes' eccentric brother was to play an important part.

The
Adventure
of the
Naval
Treaty

The Adventure of the Naval Treaty was particularly timely when it was first published. For in 1887 there actually was just such a secret treaty between England and Italy. At that time France was second only to England as a world naval power. Russia's navy ranked third. France and Russia had reached a naval agreement of their own and England quite rightly feared their combined power.

As in *The Adventure of the Blue Carbuncle* Conan Doyle features a "commissionaire" or retired soldier in this story. Here we find him working as a guard at the Foreign Office.

The Adventure of the Naval Treaty

During my school days I was friendly with a lad named Percy Phelps. He was quite brilliant and won every prize the school offered. His uncle was the well-known politician, Lord Holdhurst. I had lost contact with Phelps over the years, although I had heard that he worked in the Foreign Office. Soon after my marriage, however, I received this letter from him:

Briarbrae, Woking.

My Dear Watson,

I am sure you remember "Tadpole" Phelps, who was in school with you. You may have heard that I obtained a good job at the Foreign Office through my uncle's influence. I was in a position of trust and honor there until a horrible misfortune destroyed my career.

There is no use writing the details of that dreadful event. If you accept my request, I shall most likely tell you all about it. I have only just recovered from nine weeks of illness. Do you think that you could bring your friend, Mr. Holmes, down to see me? The police assure me that nothing more can be done. But I should like to have his opinion on the case. Do try to bring him down, and as soon as possible. Every minute seems an hour while I live in this horrible suspense. I would have contacted him sooner had I not been ill. I am still so weak that I had to dictate this letter to you. Do try and bring him.

> Your old schoolfellow,
> Percy Phelps

There was something that touched me about this letter. Phelps seemed so desperate to contact Holmes. And so I decided to lay the matter before him immediately. Within an hour I was back in our old rooms in Baker Street.

I found Holmes seated at his side table. He was wearing his dressing gown and was working hard over a chemical investigation. A large glass vessel was boiling furiously over the flame of a Bunsen burner. My friend hardly glanced up as I entered. I could see that his investigation was of some importance. So I seated myself in an armchair and waited for him to finish. Finally he brought a test tube over to the table. In his right hand he held a slip of paper.

"You come right at the moment of a crisis, Watson," said he. "If this paper remains blue, all is well. If it turns red, a man's life is lost." He dipped the paper into the test tube. It turned a dull, dirty crimson. "Hum! I thought as much!" he cried. "I will be at your service in an instant, Watson. You will find tobacco in the Persian slipper." He turned to his desk and scribbled off several telegrams. He then summoned the errand boy and instructed him to dispatch them at once. At last he threw himself down in the chair opposite me.

"A very commonplace little murder," said he.

"You've got something better, I fancy. Do you bring me news of some crime, Watson?"

I handed Sherlock Holmes the letter. He read it with great attention.

"It does not tell us much, does it?" he remarked as he handed it back to me.

"Hardly anything," I answered.

"And yet the writing is of interest."

"But the writing is not his own," I said.

"Precisely. It is a woman's," said Holmes.

"A man's surely!" I cried.

"No, a woman's; and a woman of rare character. So, we already know that your client is close to someone who, for good or evil, has an exceptional character. My interest is already awakened in this case. If you are ready, we will start at once for Woking. Let us see this friend who is in trouble and meet the lady to whom he dictates his letters."

We caught the early train. In little under an hour we found ourselves in the country. Briarbrae was within a few minutes walk of the station. It was a large house with sprawling grounds. Upon arrival we were shown into an elegantly furnished drawing room. We were soon joined by a rather stout man. His age may have been closer to forty than to thirty. But his cheeks were so red and his eyes so merry that he seemed like a plump and mischievous boy.

"I am so glad that you have come," said he. He shook our hands enthusiastically. "Percy has been asking after you all morning. Ah, poor old chap, he clings to any straw. His father and mother asked me to see you. The mere mention of the subject is painful to them."

"We have had no details yet," observed Holmes. "I perceive that you are not yourself a member of the family."

Our acquaintance looked surprised. Then he glanced down and began to laugh.

"Of course, you saw the 'J.H.' on my shirt," said he. "For a moment I thought you had done something clever. Joseph Harrison is my name. Percy is to marry my sister Annie. You will find her in his room. She has nursed him hand and foot these last two months. Perhaps we had better go in at once. I know how impatient Percy is."

He showed us into another room on the same floor. It was furnished partly as a sitting room and partly as a bedroom. Flowers were arranged in every nook and corner. A young man was lying on the sofa. He was very pale and worn. A woman was sitting beside him. She rose as we entered.

"Shall I leave, Percy?" she asked.

He clutched her hand to make her stay.

"How are you, Watson?" said he. "I should never have known you under that moustache. I probably look different too. This, I presume, is your celebrated friend, Mr. Sherlock Holmes?"

I introduced him and we both sat down. The stout young man had left us, but his sister still remained. She was a striking-looking woman with large dark eyes and thick black hair. Her dark coloring made Percy's face look even more pale.

"I won't waste your time," said he. "I'll plunge right into the matter. I was a happy and successful man, Mr. Holmes. I had a very good job working in the Foreign

Office. As you may know, the Foreign Office is where major dealings are made with foreign countries. Through the influence of my uncle, Lord Holdhurst, I rose rapidly to a responsible position. When my uncle became Foreign Minister, he gave me several jobs of great trust. Each one I completed successfully. At last he came to have the utmost confidence in my work and trust.

"Nearly ten weeks ago—to be more exact, on the 23rd of May—he called me into his private room. He first complimented me on the good work I had done. He then informed me that he had a new assignment for me.

"He took out a gray roll of paper from his bureau. 'This is the original secret treaty between England and Italy. You probably have heard rumors about its existence. I regret to say that there has been some talk of it in the papers. It is of enormous importance that nothing further leak out. The French or Russian embassies would pay an immense sum to learn the contents of these papers. The treaty should not leave my bureau, but it is necessary for them to be copied. Do you have a desk in your office?'

" 'Yes, sir,' I answered.

" 'Then take the treaty and lock it up there. I shall give directions that you may remain after everyone else leaves for the day. You can then copy it without fear of being seen. When you have finished, relock both the original and your copy in the desk. Hand them over to me personally tomorrow morning.'

"I took the papers and—"

"Excuse me an instant," said Holmes. "Were you alone during this conversation?"

"Absolutely," answered Phelps.

"In a large room?"

"Thirty feet each way."

"In the center?"

"Yes, about it."

"And speaking low?"

"My uncle's voice is always remarkably low. I hardly spoke at all."

"Thank you," said Holmes, shutting his eyes. "Please go on."

"I did exactly what he had said. I waited until the other clerks had left. One of them, Charles Gorot, was behind in his work and remained. So I left him there and went out for dinner. When I returned he was gone. I plunged right into my task. I wanted to finish as quickly as possible. Joseph—the Mr. Harrison you just met—was in town. He was going to travel down to Woking on the eleven o'clock train. I hoped to join him.

"Then I examined the treaty. I saw that it was indeed of the greatest importance. It dealt with Britain's position toward Italy in the event of a French naval attack. I glanced over it and settled down to my task of copying.

"It was a long document and contained twenty-six separate articles. I copied as quickly as I could. At nine o'clock I had only done nine. It seemed hopeless for me to try to catch my train. I was beginning to feel drowsy. A cup of coffee would clear my brain. A commissionaire remains all night in a little room at the foot of the stairs. He always has a kettle on for those who are working overtime. I rang the bell to summon him.

"To my surprise, it was a woman who came. She was a large, coarse-faced, elderly woman in an apron.

She explained that she was the commissionaire's wife and cleaned the offices. I asked her to bring me some coffee.

"I wrote two more articles. Then I rose and walked up and down the room to stretch my legs. My coffee had not come and I wondered what the delay could be. I opened the door and started down the corridor to find out. There was a straight passage which led from my room. It was the only exit and was dimly lit. It ended in a curving staircase. The commissionaire's room was at the bottom. Halfway down this staircase is a small landing. Another passage runs into it. This second passage leads down a steep stair to a side door used by the servants. It is also a shortcut used by clerks coming from Charles Street. Here is a rough chart of the place."

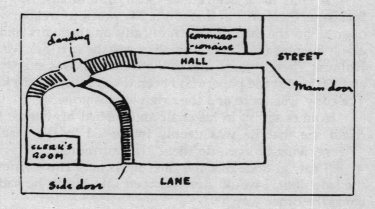

"Thank you. I think I quite follow you," said Sherlock Holmes.

"It is of the utmost importance that you make note

of this point. I went down the stairs and into the commissionaire's small room. I found him fast asleep. The kettle was boiling furiously and the water was spurting out all over the floor. I put out my hand to shake him. Suddenly the bell over his head rang loudly. He woke with a start.

" 'Mr. Phelps, sir!' said he.

" 'I came down to see if my coffee was ready.'

" 'I was boiling the kettle when I fell asleep, sir.' He looked at me and then up at the still quivering bell. There was an ever growing look of astonishment upon his face.

" 'If you are here, sir, then who rang the bell?' he asked.

" 'The bell!' I said. 'What bell is it?'

" 'It's the bell of the room you were working in.'

"A cold hand seemed to close around my heart. Someone, then, was in that room. My precious treaty lay open upon the table! I ran frantically up the stairs and along the passage. There was no one in the corridor, Mr. Holmes. There was no one in the room. All was exactly as I left it. But the papers had been taken from the desk. The copy was there and the original was gone."

Holmes sat up in his chair and rubbed his hands. I could see that he was deeply interested in the case. "Please, what did you do then?" he murmured.

"I saw at once that the thief must have come from the side door. I would have bumped into him if he had come the other way."

"Could he have been hiding in the room or in the corridor? You just said that it was dimly lit," said Sherlock.

"It is absolutely impossible. A rat could not hide in the room or the corridor. There is no cover at all," replied Percy Phelps.

"Thank you. Please proceed."

"The commissionaire had seen by my pale face that something was wrong. Therefore, he had followed me upstairs. Now we both rushed along the corridor and down the steep stairs which led to Charles Street. The door at the bottom was closed but unlocked. We flung it open and rushed out. Just then a neighboring church bell rang three times. It was a quarter to ten."

"That is of enormous importance," said Holmes. He made a note of it upon his shirtcuff.

"The night was very dark and a thin warm rain was falling. There was no one in Charles Street. We rushed along the pavement. At the far corner we found a policeman.

" 'A robbery has been committed,' I gasped. 'A document of immense value has been stolen from the Foreign Office. Has anyone passed this way?'

" 'I have been standing here for a quarter of an hour, sir,' said he. 'Only one person has passed during that time—an elderly woman with a Paisley shawl.'

" 'Ah, that is only my wife,' cried the commissionaire. 'Has no one else passed?'

" 'No one.'

" 'Then the thief must have gone the other way,' cried the commissionaire, tugging at my sleeve.

"But I was not satisfied. The attempts that he made to draw me away only increased my suspicions.

" 'Which way did the woman go?' I cried.

" 'I don't know, sir. I noticed her pass, but I had no special reason for watching her. She seemed to be in a hurry.'

" 'How long ago was it?'

" 'Oh, not very many minutes,' said the policeman.

" 'You're only wasting your time, sir. Every minute now is important,' cried the commissionaire. 'Take my word for it that my old woman has nothing to do with it. Come down to the other end of the street. Well, if you won't, I will.' And with that he rushed off in the other direction.

"But I was after him in an instant and caught him by the sleeve.

" 'Where do you live?' I asked.

" '16 Ivy Lane, Brixton,' he answered. 'But don't let yourself be misled, Mr. Phelps. Come to the other end of the street. Let us see if we can learn anything there.'

"Nothing was to be lost by following his advice. So we all three hurried down. The street was full of traffic. People were coming and going. Everyone was rushing about, eager to get out of the rain. No one could tell us who had passed.

"Then we returned to the office. We searched the stairs and the passage, but found nothing. The corridor which led to my room had a linoleum flooring. It is white and shows tracks easily. We examined it carefully but found no footprints.

"Had it been raining all evening?" asked Holmes.

"Since about seven," answered our client.

"The woman came into your room about nine. How is it that she left no traces with her muddy boots?"

"I am glad you raise that point. It occurred to me at the time. The cleaning ladies take off their boots at the commissionaire's office and put on slippers."

"I see. There were no marks on the floor even though it was raining. What did you do next?"

"We examined the room. The windows are thirty feet from the ground. Both of them were fastened from the inside. The carpet prevents any possibility of a trap door. And the ceiling is of the ordinary white-washed kind. I will pledge my life that the thief came through the door."

"How about the fireplace?"

"There is none. There is only a stove. The bell-rope hangs from a wire just to the right of my desk. Whoever rang it must have come right up to the desk. But why should any criminal wish to ring the bell? It is all a mystery."

"Certainly the case is unusual," said Holmes. "What were your next steps? Did you examine the room to see if the thief left any traces—a cigar end, a dropped glove, a hairpin, or other trifle?"

"There was nothing of the sort," answered Phelps.

"No smell?"

"Well, we never thought of that."

"Ah, the scent of tobacco would have told us a great deal."

"I never smoke myself. I think I would have noticed the smell of tobacco. There was absolutely no clue of any kind. The only fact was that the commissionaire's wife—Mrs. Tangey by name—had hurried from the place. He could give no explanation except that this was the time she usually went home. The policeman and I agreed that our best plan was to seize the woman before she got rid of the papers, if she in fact had them.

"The alarm had reached Scotland Yard by this time. Mr. Forbes, the detective, came round at once. He took up the case with a good deal of energy. We hired a cab and went to the Tangey's address. A young woman opened the door. She turned out to be Mrs. Tangey's eldest daughter. Her mother had not come back yet. We were shown into the front room to wait.

"About ten minutes later a knock came at the door. Here we made a serious mistake. Instead of opening the door ourselves, we allowed the girl to do so. We heard her say, 'Mother, there are two men in the house waiting to see you.' Then we heard the patter of feet rushing down the passage. Forbes flung open the door and we both ran into the back kitchen. The woman had got there before us. She stared at us with daring eyes. Then she suddenly recognized me. An expression of absolute astonishment came over her face.

" 'Why if it isn't Mr. Phelps of the office!' she cried.

" 'Come, come. Who did you think we were when you ran away from us?' asked my companion.

" 'I thought you were the bill collectors,' said she.

" 'That's not quite good enough,' answered Forbes. 'We have reason to believe that you have taken a paper of importance from the Foreign Office. And that you ran here to get rid of it. You must come back with us to Scotland Yard to be searched.'

"She protested and resisted. But a cab was brought and all three of us drove back in it. We had made an examination of the kitchen fire. She had not thrown any paper into it. When we reached Scotland Yard she was handed to the female searcher. I waited in an agony of suspense until she brought back her report. There was no sign of the treaty.

"Suddenly I realized the horror of my situation. Up until then I had been busy trying to find the culprit. I had been sure that I would regain the treaty. I had not dared to think about what would happen if it was lost. But now there was nothing to be done and I had time to think about my situation. It was horrible! Watson there will tell you that I was a sensitive boy at school. It is my nature. I thought about my uncle, and his high-ranking colleagues, of the shame which I had brought upon him and upon myself and on everyone who knew me. It made no difference that I was the victim of an extraordinary accident. No allowance would be made for accidents. National interests were at stake! I was ruined, shamefully, hopelessly ruined! I don't know what I did. I fancy I must have made a scene. I have a dim recollection of a group of officials crowded around me. They were trying to soothe me. One of them drove me to the train station and saw that I got on board. He would have gone with me, but my neighbor, Dr. Ferrier, was going home by that very train. He took charge of me. And it was a good thing he did. I had a fit right in the station! By the time we reached home I was practically a raving maniac.

"Everyone was roused from their beds. Poor Annie here and my mother were broken-hearted to see me in that condition. Dr. Ferrier had heard a little of the story from the detective at the station. This he told the family, which did not make matters any better. It was clear to all that I was in for a long illness. Joseph was put out of this cheery bedroom and it was turned into a sickroom for me. Here I have lain, Mr. Holmes, for over nine weeks—unconscious and raving with fever. If it had not been for Miss Harrison here and for the doctor's care, I should not be speaking to you now. She has nursed me by the day and a hired nurse has nursed me by night. It was only in the last three days that my memory returned. Sometimes I wish that it never had. The first thing I did was wire Mr. Forbes. He came out straight away. He said that everything has been done but no clue has been discovered. Examination of the commissionaire and his wife has revealed nothing. Young Gorot has also been suspected by the police. He was the clerk who stayed late at the office. But nothing was found to point to him and the matter was dropped. Mr. Holmes, I turn to you as my last hope. If you fail me, my honor and my job are lost forever."

With that the invalid sank back against his cushions. His nurse quickly poured him a drink. Holmes sat silently. His eyes were closed and his head was thrown back. I knew this pose of his. He might look disinterested to a stranger, but I knew he was totally absorbed in thought.

"Your statement has been most clear," said he at last. "I have few questions to ask. There is one of the very utmost importance, however. Did you tell anyone that you had this special task to perform?"

"No one."

"Not Miss Harrison here, for example?" asked Holmes.

"No. I had not been back to Woking between getting the order and carrying it out."

"And none of your friends or family had seen you during the day?"

"None."

"Did any of them know their way around your office?"

"Oh, yes. All of them have been shown around," said Phelps.

"Still, if you said nothing to any one about the treaty, these questions are not important."

"I said nothing."

"Do you know anything about the commissionaire?" asked Holmes.

"Nothing except that he is an old soldier."

"Thank you. I have no doubt I can get details from Forbes. The police are excellent at gathering facts, though they do not always use them to advantage."

"Do you see any prospect of solving this mystery, Mr. Holmes?" Annie Harrison asked.

"Well, the case is a complicated one. But I promise to look into the matter. I will let you know anything I find out," replied my friend.

"Do you see any clues?"

"You have given me seven. Of course I must test them before I can tell you their value to the case."

"You suspect someone?" she asked.

"I suspect myself—"

"What?"

"Of coming to conclusions too rapidly," he finished.

"Then go to London and test your conclusions."

"Your advice is excellent, Miss Harrison," said

Holmes, rising. "I think, Watson, that is what we should do. Do not let yourself have false hopes, Mr. Phelps. The affair is a very tangled one."

"I shall be in a fever until I see you again," cried my old school friend.

'Well, I'll come out by the same train tomorrow. But I doubt I'll find out anything by then."

"God bless you for promising to come," cried our client. "It gives me a fresh life to know that something is being done. By the way, I have had a letter from Lord Holdhurst."

"Ha, what did he say?" asked Sherlock Holmes.

"He was cold, but not harsh. He repeated that the matter was of the utmost importance. He added that no steps would be taken about my future until my health was better and I had a chance to repair my misfortune."

"Well, that was reasonable and considerate," said Holmes. "Come, Watson, for we have a good day's work before us in town."

Mr. Joseph Harrison drove us down to the station. We soon were whirling toward London. Holmes was sunk in profound thought for most of the journey.

"That man Phelps does not drink, does he?" he asked after a while.

"I should think not," I replied.

"Nor should I. But we are bound to take every possibility into account. The poor devil has certainly got himself into very hot water. What did you think of Miss Harrison?"

"A girl of strong character," I replied.

"Yes, but she is a good sort, or I am mistaken. She and her brother are the only children of a blacksmith.

Phelps got engaged to her when traveling last winter. She came down to be introduced to his family. Her brother came with her as escort. Then came this trouble. She stayed on to nurse her lover. Her brother Joseph, being rather comfortable, stayed on too. I've been making a few inquiries of my own, you see. Today we must make some more. I think we'll start by talking with Detective Forbes."

"You said you had a clue," I mentioned.

"Well, we have several. But we can only test their value by further investigation. What we must ask ourselves is: who is it that profits by this crime? There is the French Ambassador, there is the Russian, there is whoever might sell the treaty to either of these, and there is Lord Holdhurst."

"Lord Holdhurst!"

"Well, it is certainly possible. There might be some reason why he wanted the treaty destroyed."

"Not a statesman with the honorable record of Lord Holdhurst!" I exclaimed.

"We shall see the Lord today and find out if he can tell us anything. Meanwhile, I have sent wires from Woking Station to every evening newspaper in London. This advertisement will appear in each." He handed me a sheet of paper torn from a notebook. On it was scribbled in pencil:

REWARD—for the number of a cab which dropped off a passenger at or near the door of the Foreign Office in Charles Street at a quarter to ten on May 23rd. Respond to 221B Baker Street.

"You think the thief came in a cab?" I asked.

"If not, there is no harm done. But Mr. Phelps stated that there are no hiding places in the room or the corridors. If that is so, then the thief must have come from outside. But it was a wet night. He should have left some trace of damp on the linoleum . . . unless he came in a cab. Yes, I think that we can safely deduce a cab."

"It sounds possible."

"That is one of the clues of which I spoke. It may lead us to something. And then, of course, there is the bell . . . that is the most unique feature of the case. Why should the bell ring? Was it the thief who rang it? Or was it someone trying to prevent the crime? Or was it an accident? Or was it—" Sherlock Holmes sank back in a state of intense and silent thought. It seemed to me that some new possibility had dawned upon him.

We reached London at twenty past three, ate a quick lunch, and went to Scotland Yard. Holmes had also wired Forbes and we found him waiting for us. He was a rather small, foxy man. He acted definitely cool toward us.

"I've heard of your methods, Mr. Holmes," said he. "You use all the information that the police can give you and then you finish the case and try to discredit the police."

"On the contrary," said Holmes, "out of my last fifty-three cases, my name has only appeared in four. The police have had all the credit in forty-nine. I don't blame you for not knowing this. You are young and inexperienced. But if you wish to get along in your new duties you will work with me and not against me."

The young detective changed his manner

immediately. "I'd be very glad of a hint or two," said he.

"What steps have you taken?"

"Tangey, the guard, has been shadowed. He left the army with a good reference. His wife is a bad lot, though. I fancy she knows more about this than it appears."

"Have you shadowed her?"

"We have had her followed by one of our woman officers. So far she has revealed nothing."

"I understand that bill collectors were bothering them."

"Yes, but they were paid off," answered Forbes.

"Where did the money come from?"

"That was all right. His pension was paid him."

"What explanation did she give for answering the bell when Phelps rang for coffee?"

"She said her husband was very tired and so she went in his place," said Forbes.

"Well, certainly that would agree with his being found asleep in his chair. Did you ask her why she hurried away that night? Her haste attracted the attention of the policeman."

"She was later than usual and wanted to get home."

"Did you point out to her that you and Mr. Phelps started at least twenty minutes after her and yet got to her home before her?" asked Holmes.

"She explains that by the difference in speed between a bus and a cab."

"Did she make it clear why she ran into the kitchen?"

"Because she had the money there with which to pay the bill collectors."

"She at least has an answer for everything. Did you ask her whether in leaving she met anyone or saw anyone hanging about Charles Street?"

"She saw no one but the policeman."

"Well, you seem to have cross-examined her pretty thoroughly," said Holmes. "What else have you done?"

"The clerk, Gorot, has been shadowed without result. We can find nothing against him."

"Anything else?"

"Well, we have nothing else to go on . . . no evidence of any kind."

"Have you formed any theory about how the bell rang?" asked Holmes.

"Well, I must confess that it beats me. The thief must have been pretty arrogant to go and give the alarm like that."

"Yes, it was a queer thing to do. Many thanks to you for what you have told me. If I can put the criminal into your hands, you shall hear from me. Come along, Watson!"

"Where are we going to now?" I asked as we left the office.

"We are going to interview Lord Holdhurst, the Foreign Minister and future Premier of England."

We went immediately to the Minister's chambers and were fortunate to find Lord Holdhurst in. We were instantly shown up to his chambers.

"Your name is very familiar to me, Mr. Holmes," said Lord Holdhurst. He was a tall, slender man with curly gray hair. "Of course, I know why you have come. May I ask whom you are working for?"

"Mr. Percy Phelps," answered Holmes.

"Ah, my unfortunate nephew! Our family ties make it impossible for me to protect him in any way. I fear the incident may have a very bad effect upon his career."

"But if the document is found?"

"Ah, that, of course, would be very different," he answered.

"I have one or two questions to ask you, Lord Holdhurst."

"I shall be happy to give you any information I can."

"Did you give your nephew his instructions in this room?"

"Yes."

"Then you could not have been overheard?" asked Sherlock Holmes.

"It is out of the question."

"Did you ever mention to anyone that you intended to have the document copied?"

"Never."

"You are certain of that?"

"Absolutely," said Lord Holdhurst.

"Well, since you never said so, and Mr. Phelps never said so, and nobody else knew of the matter, then the thief's presence in the room was purely accidental. He saw his chance and he took it."

The statesman smiled. "I cannot speculate on that."

"There is another very important point which I wish to discuss with you," said Holmes. "I believe you feared grave results might follow from the details of this treaty becoming known?"

"Very grave results, indeed," answered the statesman.

"And have they occurred?"

"Not yet."

"If the treaty had reached, let us say, the French or the Russian Foreign Office, wouldn't you expect to hear about it?"

"Yes."

"Ten weeks have passed and yet nothing has been heard. Is it not possible that the treaty never reached them?"

Lord Holdhurst shrugged his shoulders.

"We can hardly suppose, Mr. Holmes, that the thief took the treaty to frame it and hang it up."

"Perhaps he is waiting for a better price."

"If he waits a little longer he will get no price at all. The treaty will cease to be secret in a few months."

"That is most important," said Holmes. "Of course, it is possible that the thief has had a sudden illness."

"An attack of fever, for example?" asked the statesman.

"I did not say so," said Holmes calmly. "And now, Lord Holdhurst, we have already taken too much of your valuable time. We shall wish you good day."

"Every success to your investigation, be the criminal who it may," answered the nobleman and bowed.

Holmes and I agreed to meet the next morning to go down to Woking together. This we did. Holmes had had no answer to his advertisement and no fresh light had been thrown upon the case. We found our client still under the care of his nurse. He seemed much better than before. He rose from the sofa and greeted us without difficulty.

"Any news?" he asked, eagerly.

"My report, as I expected, is a negative one," said

Holmes. "I have seen Forbes and I have seen your uncle. I also have a few leads which may develop into something."

"You have not lost heart, then?" Phelps asked.

"By no means."

"God bless you for saying that!" cried Miss Harrison. "If we keep our courage and our patience, the truth is bound to come out."

"We have more to tell you than you have for us," said Phelps.

"I hoped you might have something."

"Yes, we have had an adventure during the night. It might have proved quite serious, in fact." His expression grew very grave as he spoke. A look close to fear sprang up in his eyes. "Do you know," said he, "that I begin to think that I am center of some monstrous conspiracy. I think my life is in as much danger as my honor!"

"Ah!" cried Holmes.

"Last night was the first night that I slept without a nurse in the room. I did have a nightlight burning, however. Well, I had trouble sleeping. About two in the morning I heard a slight noise. It was like the sound of a mouse gnawing at a plank. I lay listening to it for some time. Then it grew louder. There was a sharp metallic sound from the window. I sat up in amazement. There could be no doubt what the sounds were now. The faint ones had been caused by someone forcing an instrument between the window and the wall. The second was the catch being lifted up.

"There was a pause then for about ten minutes. It was as if the person was waiting to see if the noise had awakened me. Then I heard a gentle creaking as the

window was very slowly opened. I could stand it no longer. I sprang out of the bed and flung open the shutters. A man was crouching at the window. He was gone in a flash. I saw little of him. He was wrapped in some sort of cloak, which came across the lower part of his face. I am sure that he had some weapon in his hand. It looked to me like a long knife. I distinctly saw the gleam of it as he turned to run."

"This is most interesting," said Holmes. "Please, what did you do then?"

"I should have followed him through the open window. But I am not strong. So I rang the bell to rouse the house. No one came at first. The bell rings in the kitchen, but the servants all sleep upstairs. And so I shouted. This brought Joseph. He then woke the others. Joseph and the groom found marks on the flower bed outside the window. But the weather has been so dry lately that they could find no tracks in the grass. They also found some marks on the fence near the road. I have said nothing to the local police. I thought it best to speak with you first."

This tale seemed to have an extraordinary effect on Sherlock Holmes. He rose from his chair and paced about the room in uncontrollable excitement.

"Do you think you could walk around the house with me?" asked Holmes of Phelps.

"Oh yes, I should like a little sunshine. Joseph will come too."

"And I also," said Miss Harrison.

"I am afraid not," said Holmes. "I think I must ask you to remain sitting exactly where you are."

The young lady sat back down. Her brother,

however, had joined us and we set off together. We passed around the lawn to the outside of Phelp's window. There were indeed, marks upon the flower bed. However, they were hopelessly vague and blurred. Holmes stopped and looked at them for an instant. Then he rose and shrugged his shoulders.

"I don't think anyone can make much of this," said he. "Let us go around the house and see why the burglar chose this particular room. I should have thought the larger windows of the dining room and drawing room would have been easier for him."

"They can be seen more clearly from the road," suggested Mr. Joseph Harrison.

"Ah, yes, of course. There is a door here he might have tried to open. What is it for?" asked Holmes.

"It is the side entrance for the tradespeople. Of course, it is locked at night," answered Phelps.

"Have you ever had anything like this happen here before?"

"Never," said our client.

"Do you keep silver in the house, or anything else to attract burglars?"

"Nothing of value."

Holmes strolled around the house with his hands in his pockets.

"By the way," said he to Joseph Harrison, "you found some place, I understand, where the fellow scaled the fence. Let us have a look at that."

Harrison led us the spot. The top of one of the wooden rails had been cracked. A small piece of the wood was hanging down. Holmes pulled it off and examined it carefully.

"Do you think that was done last night? It looks rather old, doesn't it?"

"Well, possibly so," said Harrison.

"There are no marks of anyone jumping down onto the other side. No, I fancy we shall learn nothing here. Let us go back to the bedroom and talk the matter over."

Percy Phelps was walking very slowly. He was leaning on his future brother-in-law's arm. Holmes walked swiftly across the lawn. We were at the open window of the bedroom long before the others came up.

"Miss Harrison," said Holmes. He spoke most intensely. "You must stay where you are all day. Let nothing prevent you from staying where you are. It is of the utmost importance."

"Certainly, if you wish, Mr. Holmes," said the girl in astonishment.

"When you go to bed lock the door of this room on the outside and keep the key. Promise to do this."

"But Percy?"

"He will come to London with us."

"And I am to remain here?"

"It is for his sake. You can serve him. Quick! Promise!"

She gave a quick nod of assent just as the other two came up.

"Why do you sit moping there, Annie?" cried her brother. "Come out into the sunshine!"

"No, thank you, Joseph. I have a slight headache. This room is deliciously cool and soothing."

"What do you propose now, Mr. Holmes?" asked our client.

"We must not lose sight of our main case. It would

be a great help if you would come up to London with us."

"At once?"

"Well, as soon as you can. Say in an hour," replied Sherlock Holmes.

"I feel strong enough, if I can really be of any help."

"The greatest possible."

"Perhaps you would like me to stay over there tonight?" Phelps asked.

"I was just going to propose it."

"Then if my friend of last night comes, he will find the bird flown. We are all in your hands, Mr. Holmes. You must tell us exactly what you want done. Perhaps you would prefer that Joseph come with us. He could look after me."

"Oh, no, my friend Watson is a medical man, you know. We'll have lunch here, and then we'll set off for town together."

It was arranged as he suggested, though Miss Harrison excused herself from leaving the bedroom. I could not imagine what the object of Holmes' plans were ... unless it was to keep the lady away from Phelps. Holmes had yet another surprise in store. We three went down to the train together. Holmes then calmly announced that he had no intention of leaving Woking.

"There are one or two small points which I should like to clear up before I go," said he. "Your absence, Mr. Phelps, will help me. Watson, when you reach London please take Mr. Phelps to Baker Street. Wait with him for my return. It is a good thing that you are old school friends. I am sure there is much for you to talk over. Mr.

Phelps can have the spare bedroom tonight. I will be with you in time for breakfast."

"But how about our investigation in London?" asked Phelps.

"We can do that tomorrow. I can do more for you here."

The train began to move. "Please tell them at Briarbrae that I'll be back tomorrow night," cried Phelps.

"I hardly expect to go back to Briarbrae," answered Holmes. He waved his hand to us cheerily as we shot out of the station.

Neither Phelps nor I could understand why Holmes had stayed behind.

"I suppose he wants to find out some clue as to the burglary last night—if it was indeed a burglary. For myself, I don't believe it was an ordinary thief," said Percy.

"What is your idea?" I asked.

"Perhaps I am still ill. But it seems to me that there is some deep political intrigue going on around me. For some reason I do not understand it. It sounds crazy, but consider the facts. Why should a thief try to break in at a bedroom window? There could be no hope of silver in the room. And why should he come with a long knife in his hand?"

"You are sure about that?" I asked.

"It was a knife. I saw the flash of the blade quite distinctly."

"But why on earth should someone want to kill you?"

"Ah, that is the question," Phelps said.

"Well, if a man did threaten your life last night, then perhaps Holmes will capture the man tonight. If he does we will be close to solving this mystery. It is absurd to think that you have two enemies—one who robs you while the other threatens your life."

"But Mr. Holmes said that he was not going to Briarbrae."

"I have known him for some time," said I. "I have never known him to do anything without a good reason."

That night I lay tossing and turning, brooding over this strange mystery. I invented a hundred theories. Each was more impossible than the last. Why had Holmes remained at Woking? Why had he asked Miss Harrison to remain in the sick room all day? Why hadn't he told them that he planned to stay there? I fell asleep, still trying to find the right theory.

It was seven o'clock when I awoke. I set off at once for Phelp's room. He, too, had spent a sleepless night. His first question was whether Holmes had arrived yet.

"He'll be here when he promised," said I. "And not an instant sooner or later."

My words were true. Shortly after eight a cab stopped at the door. We stood at the window and looked on. Holmes got out. His left hand was wrapped in a bandage. His face was grim and pale. He entered the house, but it was some time before he came upstairs.

"He looks like a beaten man," cried Phelps.

I was forced to confess that he was right.

"You are not wounded, Holmes?" I asked when my friend entered the room.

"Tut, it is only a scratch. Mr. Phelps, this case is certainly one of the darkest cases I have ever investigated."

"I feared that you would find it beyond you," Phelps said.

"It has been a most remarkable experience."

"That bandage tells of adventures," said I. "Won't you tell us what has happened?"

"After breakfast, my dear Watson. I suppose there has been no answer to my cabman advertisement? Well, we cannot expect to score every time."

The table was laid and Mrs. Hudson soon came in with the tea and coffee. A few minutes later she brought three covered platters. We all drew up to the table. Holmes was starving, I was curious, and Phelps was in the gloomiest state of depression.

Holmes uncovered a dish of curried chicken. "Mrs. Hudson's cooking is a little limited. But she does make a fine breakfast. What have you there, Watson?"

"Ham and eggs," I answered, lifting the corner of the dish before me.

"Good! What are you going to take, Mr. Phelps? Curried chicken, or eggs, or will you help yourself?"

"Thank you, I can eat nothing," said Phelps.

"Oh, come! Try the dish before you."

"Thank you. I would really rather not."

"Well, then," said Holmes with a mischievous grin. "Would you mind helping me?"

Phelps raised the cover of the dish. As he did he uttered a scream. He sat there staring at the plate. Across it lay a roll of blue-gray paper. He picked it up, and hugged it to him. He started dancing about the room, shrieking with delight. Then he fell back faintly into an armchair.

"There! There!" said Holmes. "I shouldn't have surprised you so. I can never resist the dramatic."

Phelps seized his hand and kissed it. "God bless you!" he cried. "You have saved my honor!"

"Well, my own was at stake as well, you know," said Holmes. "I don't like to fail at my work either."

Phelps tucked his precious document into the innermost pocket of his coat.

"I will not interrupt your breakfast further. But I am dying to know how you got the treaty!"

Sherlock Holmes swallowed a cup of coffee and ate some ham and eggs. Then he rose, lit his pipe, and settled himself down into his chair.

"I will tell you what I did first, and then I'll tell you how I came to do it," said he. "I left you at the station and then went for a walk through the country. I had tea at an inn and ordered some sandwiches for later. I remained at the inn until evening. Then I set off for Woking. I was on the main road outside Briarbrae just after sunset. When the road was clear, I climbed over the fence onto the grounds."

"Surely the gate was open?" exclaimed Phelps.

"Yes; but I did not want anyone in the house to see me. I crouched down among the bushes and crawled from one to the other. Finally I reached the hedge just opposite your bedroom window. There I squatted down and waited.

"The blind was not drawn in your room. I could see

Miss Harrison. She was reading. At a quarter past ten she closed her book. Then she fastened the shutters and left the room. I heard her shut the door. I feel sure she turned the key in the lock as well."

"The key?" asked Phelps.

"Yes. I had told Miss Harrison to lock the door and take the key with her when she went to bed. She carried out every one of my instructions. Without her cooperation you wouldn't have your papers. Soon after the lights went out. I was left squatting behind the bush.

"The night was fine, but it was a very long wait. Of course, I felt the excitement a sportsman feels waiting for the big game. There was a church clock down at Woking and it struck the quarter hours. At times the minutes seemed so long that I thought the clock had stopped. But at two in the morning, I heard a sound. A bolt was being pushed back and a key was turning in a lock. A moment later the servant's door opened. Mr. Joseph Harrison stepped out into the moonlight."

"Joseph!" cried Phelps.

Sherlock Holmes continued. "He had a black cloak thrown over his shoulder, so that he could hide his face in an instant. He walked on tip-toe in the shadows. He used his knife to unlock the window. Then he flung it open and threw back the shutters.

"I had a perfect view of the room. I could see every one of his movements. He lit two candles which stood on the mantelpiece. Then he turned back the corner of the carpet nearest the door. He stooped down and picked up a square piece of board. Out of this hiding place he took that little roll of paper. He pushed down the board, rearranged the carpet, and blew out the candles. I stood waiting for him outside the window. He climbed out the window and walked straight into my arms.

"Well, he flew at me with the knife. I got this cut over my knuckles before I gained control. Eventually, he listened to reason and gave up the papers. Having got them, I let him go. I wired Forbes this morning. If he is quick enough to catch his bird, well and good! But if he finds the nest empty, all the better for the government. I think Lord Holdhurst and Mr. Percy Phelps would prefer this case not to go to court."

"My God!" gasped our client. "The stolen papers were in the room with me all this time?"

"So it was."

"And Joseph! Joseph is a villain and a thief!" exclaimed Phelps.

"Hum! I am afraid Joseph was more dangerous than he seemed. I spoke with him this morning and I learned that he lost heavily on stocks and would do just about anything for money. He is an absolutely selfish man. Your treaty was a chance for a fortune. He did not allow his sister's happiness or your reputation to stand in his way."

Percy Phelps sank back in his chair.

"My head whirls," said he, "your words have dazed me!"

"The main problem was that there was too much evidence," said Sherlock Holmes. "I had to pick out the most important facts. Then I had to piece them together. I had already begun to suspect Joseph. He had intended to travel with you that night. He easily could have called for you on his way to the station. Then I heard that someone had tried to get into the bedroom. It had been Joseph's room before the incident. Your sudden arrival with the doctor had put him out. The attempt had been made on the first night that a nurse was absent. This showed that the intruder knew the ways of the house. It had to be Joseph!"

"How blind I have been!" exclaimed our client.

"The facts of the case are these: This Joseph Harrison entered the office through the Charles Street door. He knew his way and so walked straight up to your room. You had just left in search of your coffee. He found no one there and so rang the bell. At that instant his eyes caught sight of the paper on the table. A glance showed him a State document of immense value lay before him. In an instant he thrust it into his pocket and was gone. A few minutes passed before the sleepy guard drew your attention to the bell. That was just enough time for him to make his escape.

"He made his way to Woking by the first train. He concealed his prize in a very safe place. He intended to take it to the French Embassy or Russian Embassy within a day or two. Then came your sudden return. He was bundled out of his room. From that time on there were always two people in the room. He could not get at his treasure. The situation must have been maddening. But at last he saw his chance. He tried to break in, but you were awake and he had to flee.

"I already knew that the papers were in the room, but I had no desire to rip up all the planking in search of them. I would let him take them from their place for me.

So I arranged for you to be away and for Miss Harrison to be in the room all day. This was to keep him from breaking in before I got back. Is there any other point which I can make clear?"

"Why did he try to get in by the window?" I asked. "He could have entered by the door."

"To reach the door he would have had to pass seven bedrooms. On the other hand he could get out onto the lawn with ease. Anything else?"

"You do not think that he meant to kill me?" asked Phelps. "The knife was only meant as a tool."

"It may be so," answered Sherlock Holmes, "but that is one deduction I would not like to test."

BOOK ONE

Sir Arthur Conan Doyle's

THE ADVENTURES OF
SHERLOCK HOLMES

Adapted for young readers by Catherine Edwards Sadler

A Study In Scarlet In the first Sherlock Holmes story ever written, Holmes and Watson embark on their first case together—an intriguing murder mystery.

The Red-headed League Holmes comes to the rescue in a most unusual heist!

The Man With The Twisted Lip Is this a case of murder, kidnapping, or something totally unexpected?

Join the uncanny and extraordinary Sherlock Holmes, and his friend and chronicler, Dr. Watson as they tackle dangerous crimes and untangle the most intricate mysteries.

AVON **C** CAMELOT

**AN AVON CAMELOT ORIGINAL • $2.95 U.S./$3.50 Can.
(ISBN: 0-380-78089-5)**

BOOK THREE

Sir Arthur Conan Doyle's
THE ADVENTURES OF
SHERLOCK HOLMES

Adapted for young readers by Catherine Edwards Sadler

The Adventure of the Engineer's Thumb When a young engineer arrives in Dr. Watson's office with his thumb missing, it leads to a mystery in a secret mansion, and a ring of deadly criminals.

The Adventure of the Beryl Coronet Holmes is sure that an accused jewel thief is innocent, but will he be able to prove it?

The Adventure of Silver Blaze Where is Silver Blaze, a favored racehorse which has vanished before a big race?

The Adventure of the Musgrave Ritual A family ritual handed down from generation to generation seemed to be mere mumbo-jumbo—until a butler disappears and a house maid goes mad.

Join the uncanny and extraordinary Sherlock Holmes, and his friend and chronicler, Dr. Watson, as they tackle dangerous crimes and untangle the most intricate mysteries.

AVON **C** CAMELOT

AN AVON CAMELOT ORIGINAL • $2.95 U.S./$3.50 Can.
(ISBN: 0-380-78105-0)

Sherlock 3–8/89